# The Burning Magical Star!

With a last impatient jerk he had it open. Then he edged out its contents almost as if he expected something to bite him. Monnie squeezed her hands together and tried again to yell at him to let it alone—that there was going to be bad trouble. She was as sure of that as she was that she stood there shaking in the cold of the night.

Whatever was in the envelope did not come out easily. Bim had to pull and pry at it. Then he worked it loose at last and held it up. It was not another mirror as Monnie had half feared it might be. Instead Bim held a star—a five-pointed star—or rather the outline of one, for it appeared to be made of wire.

The wire blazed with so bright a fire that Monnie heard Bim's gasp as he let it fall to the ground. Then . . .

# SEVEN SPELLS TO SUNDAY

## ANDRE NORTON
## AND PHYLLIS MILLER

PUBLISHED BY POCKET BOOKS NEW YORK

POCKET BOOKS, a Simon & Schuster division of
GULF & WESTERN CORPORATION
1230 Avenue of the Americas, New York, N.Y. 10020

ISBN: 0-671-56086-7

First Pocket Books printing October, 1980

10 9 8 7 6 5 4 3 2 1

AN ARCHWAY PAPERBACK and ARCH are trademarks
of Simon & Schuster.

Printed in the U.S.A.

# Contents

# 1

## Monnie's Here—So's Bim!

Monnie squatted down on her heels and worked with both hands to pull the felt-tip pen-marker out of the hip pocket of her dirty jeans. It was a very tight fit and it had leaked—leaving a big red mark on the outside.

Hoping there was enough of the goop still left in the pen part to use, she poked a finger hard against the marker tip and got a faint pinkish stain back. Then she wiped her hand across her knee absentmindedly and looked closely at what lay, one side up, on the ground before her.

This crummy old lot where everybody dumped stuff was always messed up with all kinds of junk. But this was the first time Monnie had ever seen a mailbox left here. It was a big one,

1

too. And the top was all bent in as if somebody had taken a baseball bat or something like that and tried to pound it to bits.

But it sure was strong. You could still force the front cover closed and even pull up the flag part which showed there was mail inside—if you worked hard enough.

She twirled the pen between two fingers and studied the box very carefully. One block over was the housing project. There were mailboxes there, sure. But they were the small kind set into the wall of the apartment hall, and lots of them had their doors pulled off and broken. They weren't much good for anything any more.

Monnie had never seen one this big and not the wall kind. Except in a picture once—a picture on a Christmas card. Then it had been set out in the country someplace, and there had been a wreath hanging on it and a lot of snow piled all around the pole on which it was fastened.

She reached out to touch the battered side of the mailbox. It was sure a funny color—someone had painted it purplish—not bright purple. Or else it had been lying here so long the sun had faded the color. And there was no number on it.

Holding the barrel of the felt pen between her teeth, Monnie now used both hands to turn the box over and set it up straight. She gathered some old bricks to steady it into place. Then, for the first time, she saw that there *was* something

painted on the bent front after all. Stars—one—
two. . . . She counted as she touched each one—
seven of them, all in a row from top to bottom.
They were so dim she could hardly make out their
shapes but they *were* stars. Now why stars when
there were no numbers, no name? That did not
really matter though.

With the pen still in her mouth she set about
collecting one or two more bricks, wedging the
box even tighter so it could not fall over again.
Then she pulled at the flag. In spite of the dents
and bulges in the box, it could still be moved
up and down.

This was a good place to leave it. There was
an old, rusting car between it and the path that
cut across to the project, and some tall, dried-
up weeds to hide it more. Yes—Monnie looked
around carefully, her eyes narrowed and searching—she had picked out just about the best
place for it.

Now she leaned forward. The sun was out but
it was chilly when the wind blew this way. Her
hands were cold and she hunched her shoulders
under the jacket Mrs. Johnson had put out for
her. It was a little too small, but she supposed
she'd never have anything that really fitted. At
least not until she was old enough to leave school
and get a real job so she had some money of
her own.

For a minute or two Monnie thought of being

a waitress like Stella—'course she was always talking about how her feet nearly killed her and how stingy the tips were. Or perhaps she could get a place in the bakery. Monnie sniffed deeply—she could almost smell chocolate frosting and spice buns. Only you had to be old—it seemed like everything good only came when you were old.

And what was she doing here now anyway? This was silly, little-kid stuff. For a moment she was ready to jam the pen back into her pocket again, send the mailbox flying with a good hard kick. But something would not let her.

It was queer how she had felt ever since yesterday when she had found the box—like it was important, though no mailbox could ever be important to her, Monnie Fitts. There was no one in this whole wide world who was going to write *her* a letter—or even send her a throwaway folder. She was herself—one—alone. She guessed she could just get up and walk away out of this lot and nobody would care much.

Oh, Miss Reeder—she might come around asking the Johnsons where Monnie Fitts was, for a while. Probably she'd be glad. Any girl nine-going-fast-on-ten who'd been in as many foster homes as Monnie had was sure a pain and one Miss Reeder would be glad to get rid of, if she told the truth.

And the Johnsons—well, they had that old

4

Bim Ross, and their daughter Stella they were always bragging on:

"Stella got A's—Stella never did that when she was your age—Stella. . . ." Monnie gathered a goodish ball of spit in her mouth and let it fly. She had half meant to hit the box, but missed, to plaster a weed stem instead.

If she only had a little cash money she would sure light out of here, she sure would!

Why was she sitting here then thinking about the box and mail she was never going to get? She was no little kid to keep hoping things were ever going to be any different—she knew better.

But even as she thought so, she began to use the pen, lettering on the box slowly and with all the care she could:

"M-o-n-n-i-e"

And then, a little crooked because there was not so much space left there at the top and she had to put one "t" a little below:

"F-i-t-t-s"

She had been careful not to run over the lines of any of the pale stars, and the red did look bright against the faded purple. Monnie laid the pen down and worked at the flag until it stood upright. Then out of the front of her jacket she brought the folded piece of paper. She had had no chance to get any real writing paper, of course. They would have wanted to know why she wanted it. But she had torn a sheet out at the back of her school notebook and then stuck it into part of a brown paper bag, folding the bag over and around it, and fastening it down tight with tape.

Now she half crumpled it in one hand, ready even at that last minute to make it into a ball and throw it away. Kid stuff—silly old kid stuff. . . .

She didn't have to read her message again—she knew every word. The note had taken her a long time to write, because she was not a good writer—though she liked to read, even though mostly she only saw comics. It was a story in one of those that had given her the idea in the first place.

"I'm Monnie Fitts—and I want a letter. A real letter—for just me, Monnie Fitts."

Throw it away. Nobody was going to find the box—silly game. . . .

But Monnie's hands moved in spite of what she was thinking. The brown-covered note went into the box, and she pounded shut the front cover quickly. But not quickly enough. . . .

"Hey—hey, what you doin' there, Monnie?"

Monnie pushed halfway around, her back now to the box, a very ugly scowl on her thin face.

"None of your business, Bim." Her fingers crooked up ready to scratch if he tried to jump her. Of all the bad luck! He must have sneaked out and followed her.

"What you got?" He edged closer, but kept

6

one wary eye on Monnie, having tangled with her before and knowing well that she could fight and was as tough as Matt Pringle if you pushed her hard and far enough.

"What I got's my business." Monnie dared not move. Let Bim see the mailbox and her whole secret was lost. He would never let her—nor any one else he could blab it to—forget it.

"Ma Johnson's lookin' for you. She wants you to go to the store."

He was trying to wriggle his way farther to the left to see what Monnie, with her own turning body, was trying even harder to hide.

"That's a lie," she returned flatly. "She never asks me to—" Then she flushed, realizing where her unguarded tongue had led her.

"Sure, she never asks you 'cause you took the change." Bim's grin grew wider. "That was sure a dumb trick. Getting a can of cat food with it and lettin' Rosie see you feedin' that old stray—"

"She had kittens hidden—I heard 'em. And there wasn't nothing in the trash cans for her." Monnie again spoke before she thought. No use ever trying to explain a thing like that to Bim.

"Cats don't count." He laughed now. "And so what you got hiding here?"

He moved then, a quick leap forward, his hand hard against her shoulder, pushing her off-balance so she tumbled flat and he was able to see the mailbox.

7

To her surprise he did not laugh. Instead, he stared down at her find in a very odd way, with an expression on his face Monnie had never seen there before. Bim was thin and had a ragged tangle of greasy yellowish hair which he could never cram entirely under any hat. There was generally a smudge of dirt somewhere across his face. This morning a smear ran under his nose like a shadow of a mustache. And his nose itself was pink. He sniffed a lot, and it was plain he was going to have one of his bad colds.

"It's a mailbox. . . ."

Now that, thought Monnie, was a dumb thing even for Bim to say. Anybody could see what it was.

"It isn't the kind we got neither. . . ." She felt as if he was thinking aloud and not talking to her at all.

"How did it get here?"

Monnie shrugged. "How would I know? Somebody grabbed it off somewhere and then just dumped it, I guess."

Bim made no effort to touch the box. Instead he hunkered down not too far from Monnie and looked at it very carefully.

"Funny lookin' kind of thing," he observed, still as if he were talking only to himself. "It's painted a funny color—not blue or red or anything. And not. . . . And what's them?" He was pointing now to the row of seven stars on the front. "Where's the name, or the number, or whatever that oughtta be there?"

"There isn't none—just them." Monnie was no longer sure of herself. Her first impulse to fight with Bim and protect her own secret seemed to be fading. Bim wasn't laughing at her or anything. He seemed just as interested as she had been when she had first seen it.

"That's your name. Why d'ya put your name on it?"

"Why shouldn't I," she snapped. "Old beat-up mailbox, if I want to put my name on it—I guess I can. No one's goin' to say I can't."

She expected Bim to answer with something nasty and sharp like he always did. But to her surprise he was quiet for a moment and then said instead:

"No mailman's gonna come in here hunting a box—"

"I know that!"

Bim rubbed his hand under his nose adding to the black mark of his mustache smear. He sniffed.

"But it isn't no regular mailbox either. Suppose it was put here just to hide messages—real Captain Norex stuff?"

"Captain Norex." Monnie sniffed in turn, but her sound had nothing to do with a cold. "That's just a story—on TV—and in those silly old comic books."

Bim shook his head slowly. "You can't tell for

9

sure. I never heard of no purple mailbox with stars on it, neither. And I bet you haven't. There's gotta be a reason for that. And—an' I'm going to find out!"

Before Monnie could snatch it away, Bim grabbed the pen she had left lying on the ground. With lettering even more shaky and uneven than hers, he was adding in a line down along that of the stars:

"B-I-M R-O-S-S."

Monnie hurled herself at him fiercely. But this time Bim was ready for her. Doubtless he had been expecting just such an attack. With the pen still in hand he threw himself back out of her reach, scrambled along on his hands and knees, kicking out at her twice when she tried to catch hold, and then he got behind the rusted car and rose to run.

Bim could outrun her any day; he'd had plenty of practice outrunning most of the kids in the project. He had no more friends than she did, and she knew that Matt Pringle had cornered him twice and beat him up for just hanging around and making a nuisance of himself.

Slowly Monnie went back to the mailbox. There was no use in trying to smear off Bim's name. But at least he had not opened it and seen her letter. Would he come back for that? Monnie pulled hard at the cover. She had better get her

10

message out. Bim wasn't going to be able to show that around and get them all laughing at her.

Only trouble was that the harder she pulled the more the cover stuck tight shut. Well, if she could not get it open, Bim certainly would not either. Maybe she could get a screwdriver or something later and pry it loose.

Funny, when she looked at those stars down the front, they seemed brighter and more shiny. Monnie wanted to touch one but there was something so odd about that shininess that she did not quite dare.

She stood up to glance around. Bim had told the truth. She was sure no one was going to see the mailbox—not unless they knew just where it was and came hunting for it. There was no use in her sticking around here trying to get it open—not now.

Monnie squeezed past the wreck of the car and came out on the badly cracked sidewalk beyond. This was a queer piece of an old street. Once there had been houses built along it. Later some had been torn down or just fallen to pieces, while all kinds of trash had been dumped around. They had been going to build more of the project buildings out in this direction, but the money had run out or something and so this big mess had been here for years—at least as long as Mrs. Johnson said she could remember.

But there was a secret place here, too. Halfway

11

along the broken-down street, facing the lot where the mailbox now lay, there was an old wooden store. Its front windows were all smashed and pieces of the wood siding were torn away. But behind the store was something else.

There was a house back there. Monnie had found it and she was sure no one else knew about it. Or if they once had, it had been forgotten long ago. It was not made of wood like all the other half-demolished buildings on the street. No, its walls were all of big stones—not the same sizes nor shapes, yet fitted together so tightly that only a very few had fallen out.

The roof was half-gone, of course, because that *had* been wood, and there were holes in the floor. But Monnie knew them all and was very careful not to go near them. It was the shape of the house, the fact that it was so small—as if it had been made for children not grownups—that interested her the most. And she was sure it had been there a very, very long time.

There was only one big room in it but a broken ladder against one wall pointed up to a hole. She guessed that before the wooden floor above had rotted and come apart, there had perhaps been another room up there too. A large part of one wall was a big, big fireplace, and there were still some links of rusted chain hanging down over where the fire must once have burned. Monnie thought that maybe a pot might have swung there once and the people who lived there had cooked like that and not on any real stove.

Some plants with strange leaves and even stranger smells grew around the walls of the house in summer. Some smells were good, and Monnie had squashed the leaves between her fingers to sniff at them. But those were all dried up and gone now.

There was something else about the house she was trying to remember now. Looking carefully up and down to be sure she would not be sighted—especially by Bim, if he were hiding— she made a dash across to the stone house. What was it she was trying so hard to remember? Something she had seen here—something important. . . .

She tiptoed in across the rotting floor as carefully as she could. The fireplace! Yes, it was something about the fireplace! But there was nothing to see there by the dim inside light except that piece of chain.

Monnie tried to look up into the chimney itself. But that was also dark and dirty, it made her a little frightened, as if she was looking up into a kind of cage that might reach right down and grab her.

It was when she stepped back that she saw what she had so dimly remembered. Cut into the wide, long stone of the mantelpiece, half-hidden by dust

13

and powdery, rotten bits of wood fallen from the ceiling, were stars!

They were carved very deeply into the stone and Monnie had to stand on tiptoe to scrape the dust out of one to make sure she was right. Yes, it was a star! And—she counted, slowly, and carefully—there were seven of them!

The mailbox—had the mailbox come from this old, old house? She wanted to know so badly that it hurt inside her. This was like waiting in the dentist's office (which was about the worst thing Monnie could think of right then), waiting and not knowing what was going to happen next—except that it was going to be awful!

This was scary. . . . She should never have left that letter—never, never, never!

Monnie ran back to the field, around the wrecked car. But. . . .

The flag she had so carefully pushed up was down! Bim must have come back. She dug her fingers into the crack the battering had left open at the top of the box lid and jerked it forward with all her might.

The box was empty. Just wait until she got to Bim! If he dared . . . just let him dare to talk about her letter . . . just let him try!

14

# 2

---

# A Special for Monnie

Bim lay flat beside the rusty wreck of the car. He had seen Monnie slip across the street just as he had seen her go several times before. She always went to the same place—that old stone house or whatever it was. Twice he had tried to see what she was doing there, sneaking up just as quietly as he could. Only all he had then ever seen was her just standing or sitting there, her face closed up as if she was thinking of something important.

He could always tell when Monnie was thinking. Her eyes squeezed kind of tight—though not quite closed. And her mouth was a straight pink line across her face. There was a scowling V right between her thick, black eyebrows. Monnie had sort of interested him ever since that day three months ago when Miss Reeder had brought her to the Johnsons'.

She was tough, maybe near as tough in her own way as Matt Pringle—even though she was a girl. And you never knew what she might be thinking about, or even what might make her burst out into a wild, yelling fight.

Bim rolled over on his back and stared up into the sky across which there floated, not nice white clouds like the ones on TV, but trails of grayish stuff like smoke. Johnsons' place wasn't so bad. The grub was good and they didn't yell at him— much. But it was lonesome—and even worse since he had learned to keep away from Matt's gang. *They* weren't going to let him in with them—no matter how much he tried.

Most of the time after school he had to spend dodging around by himself. That was really why he had started following Monnie. Seemed like she always knew just what she wanted to do—or where to go.

But what was this mailbox thing? You put up a mailbox to get letters. Bim thought about letters. Once he had gotten a postcard. Hank Bevis sent that. Hank had had a chance to go to summer camp, year before last. He'd probably only sent it along to prove he *could* go—which was more than Bim had ever had a chance to do.

But who was going to put any mail in an old

broken box out in this dump? Or did Monnie belong to a gang maybe—a gang of spies who left
messages for each other?

Bim sat up. A secret mailbox! But if it were so
secret—why had Monnie written her name right
across it? Her name . . . ? He had written his
there, too!

Suddenly it seemed much colder and Bim
shivered. His name was written right out there
where anybody could read it—and if Monnie was
a spy or something, then those she would be working with—or for—would be looking for him, Bim
Ross!

He scuttled back around the barrier of the car.
The mailbox was still there—just as Monnie had
fixed it up with the broken bricks to hold it in
place. The flag was up. And, in what seemed very
bright, far too bright, lettering across the front,
were their names. Bim grabbed up a big handful
of dead grass and scrubbed hard at his. But not
a single letter even smeared.

What had Monnie put in the box? Maybe if he
could find out—and take it—he could make a
deal with her gang. He jerked and pulled at the
lid, but it was just as if it were locked in place.
Maybe it was—maybe there was some secret way
of opening it that only Monnie knew.

Bim looked over his shoulder. There was no
sign of her now, but some kids were coming down
the street from the alleyway—Matt and his gang.

The last thing in the world Bim wanted now was to be caught by them here in the open.

On hands and knees, he headed back for the old car, and once on the other side of it, he got up and ran, not stopping until he reached the lobby of the Johnsons' part of the project where he leaned against the stained and written-on wall, breathing in deep gasps.

But that night he continued to watch Monnie when he was sure she was not looking. What *had* she put in the box and why? From time to time he saw her watching him in turn, always with that black, angry look on her face, as if she could reach right into his mind and read what he was thinking. He went to bed so early that Mrs. Johnson came in to take his temperature and see if he had a cold. But at least Monnie was clear at the other end of the hall. And, once Mrs. Johnson had gone, Bim crept out of bed and pushed a suitcase in front of the closed door.

It was just that he did not want any surprises in the night. The very thought of the mailbox (which he could not seem to push out of his mind, no matter how hard he tried) made him feel as shivery as if he knew Matt was laying for him behind some corner. Perhaps this was even worse, because he knew just what would happen if Matt caught him, while he did not know *who* would come to that mailbox on which he had been so dumb as to put his own name!

Monnie lay very quiet in her own bunk bed. She had the top one and Stella, who came in later, was below. Usually she could put herself to sleep with the house story. She had started doing that when she had first gone to the Renfrews, and that was a long time ago now—she'd been just a little kid.

Patsy Renfrew had started it—taken her to the library for story hour and the librarian had showed them this book. It was all pictures—no reading at all—and the book had been a queer one because every other page had only been half the size of the one before. So you turned that and half the picture was different.

That was the first time Monnie had gotten in real trouble, too. She had waited until the library teacher laid the book down. And then she'd hidden it—under her coat. Mrs. Renfrew—she was mad. Took her right back to the library when she found out. The library teacher had tried to tell Mrs. Renfrew about cards and borrowing. But she wouldn't even listen—or let Monnie go with Patsy to story hour again. In fact she called Miss Reeder and said she wouldn't have any little thief in her house.

So Monnie had gone to the Abbotts. But they were not interested in libraries, and anyway she'd only been there a little time before Mrs. Abbott's mother got sick and came to live with them. Then they said they had no room for Monnie. After she had been with the Lewises and—but what did it all matter anyway. She had never stayed long any place.

It was the house in the book that did mean something. Monnie could close her eyes and re-member every part of the half-page house with all its changes. Almost every night she thought that the book was not a made-up story at all but real. And someday she'd find the house and walk in— and maybe close the door tight and then be safe and never have to move again. She planned each room—just what chair would sit here and which there. Generally she went to sleep before she was even through putting everything in place in the front room.

Then when she came here and found the stone house, it was in a way so like the book house that it scared her at first. Afterward, it changed her thinking. So now her night-house was part book, part the real one. But she never dreamed about it—it was just her own private think-thing.

Only tonight. . . .

She never heard Stella come in, she never even got near the fireplace of the think-house. In-stead. . . .

It was dark and it was cold and she was outside somewhere. There were all kinds of queer, lumpy-looking shadows around and Monnie stood very still not wanting to get too near any of them. She was listening, also, as if it were very important that she hear something. But all was very quiet—too quiet. She wanted to hear the sound of a car coming down a street, or even the distant sound of a siren from the highway to break that quiet.

Now that she had a chance to look around she knew exactly where she was and this was no think-story of hers! She stood in the trash-covered dump place. And the biggest nastiest-looking shadow was of the rusting car, as if the car was some great animal getting ready to jump right at her. But closer yet there was something else—some shiny dots a lot nearer to the ground.

When she saw them, somehow Monnie felt much better. The shadows grew smaller and did not look so queer and frightening. There were seven of those shining dots—she could count them. And they were not dots either. They were stars—seven stars set in a line! The stars on the mailbox! Now they glowed as brightly as if they were real stars in the sky—though it was cloudy tonight and not many of the real ones showed.

There was a difference in the painted stars, too. The longer Monnie looked at them the more she was sure of that. The top one shone the brightest —like it was a great big diamond. She wanted to go and touch it but somehow her feet would not work. And then. . . .

"Monnie!"

She shook her head against the demand of that call. But, in spite of her wish, she opened her eyes. There was the ceiling right up over her head. If she sat up and wasn't too careful she'd whack herself against it. And it was morning. She closed her eyes and tried to bring back the nighttime adventure which now did not appear frightening at all—just very exciting. But her efforts failed. This was morning—Monday morning—and if she did not get up and wash and dress and do all the rest she had to do every single boring morning of her life, Mrs. Johnson or Stella would be there to push her into it.

With a sigh Monnie prepared to face another Monday which would be no better than any she had ever known before. Only this time she kept on remembering that very strange dream. And— she glanced at the kitchen clock—if she really hurried she would have time to cut across the dump lot and get on the bus at the Amsterdam corner, a chance to see the mailbox again. She did that sometimes—it was a change to avoid going with Bim.

Bim. . . . She remembered the box had been opened. Did Bim have that letter of hers stuck into one of his books? He looked up, saw her watching him, and glanced hurriedly away, shoveling cereal into his mouth so fast as if he, too, wanted to get away.

But she was quicker this morning. And she dodged into the dump lot before Bim, who had been called back to pick up his forgotten lunchbox, could follow. Monnie sped straight to the mailbox, determined to get a good look at it before she had to meet the school bus.

The flag—it was up! Startled, she knelt down to fumble at the lid. Then she moved more cautiously. Perhaps Bim had planted a very unpleasant surprise inside. She tugged, and the catch, which had seemed so hard to move the day before, now gave easily. Then. . . .

A letter! A real letter. But who ever heard of a purple envelope? Monnie snatched at it and held it out into the light.

"Miss Monnie Fitts," she read almost unbelievingly. Up in the left-hand corner there was another line of words—two of them—printed in silver: "Seven Spells."

Instead of a postage stamp, there was a star on the right—a star as shining and silvery as the writing. Her own name was written in red, just as she had put it on the outside of the box.

Bim? No—of that she was certain. Where would he ever get a purple envelope, and silver ink, and a star like that? This was her own—not any trick of Bim's.

She put the envelope carefully into her wallet. No time to open it now if she were to make the bus. But she did have a letter—a real one. Her excitement over that made her feel as warm as if she were wearing at least three jackets one on top

23

of the other as she reclosed the mailbox and hurried on to the bus stop.

Ann Perry and Esther Hartmen were already there, giggling, pretending not to see her. But that did not make Monnie unhappy today. If the bus would only come! She could get a seat near the front—one to herself—and then have a chance to see. . . .

When she did have the seat, right behind Mr. Chambers, who drove, Monnie wriggled the envelope carefully out of her wallet and hunched one shoulder so, as she hoped, no one else could see. To her surprise the bright purple looked faded in this stronger light, and both the star and the silver lettering were so faint she could barely see them now. But her name was written as strong and bright as ever. She tore with her fingertip at the flap. It came open easier than she had hoped. There was a sheet of paper folded inside, wrapped around something that felt hard.

With great care Monnie held it open a little and peeked inside.

The hard thing, which was about as long as her third finger, was as silver as the star and the writing had been. At first she thought it might be a pen, but whoever saw one that queer shape. Then she saw it was a broom—a little broom. Not like those people used in houses. No—this appeared more as if some one had gathered a mass of twigs and tied them tightly to a long and rather crooked pole—a very untidy looking broom.

There were words on the paper: "Sweep clean."

One used a broom to sweep, yes. But with a broom so small and of silver, and so rough, how could she hope to sweep anything? Frowning over the problem, which seemed far more important than any she might have to face in class that day, Monnie rewrapped the broom in the covering paper, folded the envelope as tightly about it as she could and crammed the whole thing back into her wallet, just as Selma Lang slumped down in the seat beside her.

Selma did not look any more pleased at having to share Monnie's seat than Monnie herself felt. She was a small girl with rabbity teeth who chewed her nails and could talk about nothing but the latest song hits. Now she wriggled in her seat and, having no better audience than Monnie, demanded:

"Did 'ja hear the Bats last night? They were on ADJW more'n an hour. M'dad said he'd take a hammer to m' transistor if I didn't cut 'em off. I went on in Jamie's room though—Jamie was sleeping over at Ruth's. And so I got to hear the whole show. It was super-super!"

"I don't have a radio," Monnie returned shortly.

"No, I suppose you don't!" Selma agreed.

Monnie bristled. Selma's tone suggested that Monnie Fitts could not expect to own the better things of life—such as a transistor over which one could hear the popular songs screamed by the Bats and other groups. But the thought of what lay in her wallet kept her from the sharp answer she might have made. Selma Lang did not have a silver brush broom.

It was a queer day, Monnie discovered. Though she was used to things going wrong, it was seldom that there were days when everything went right. In fact, looking back in wonderment once or twice during the following hours, she could not remember any such before.

Today, in social studies, she could not remember the answer to a sudden quiz and out of nowhere there came the tiny picture of a broom sweeping. And, where it swept clean, there was another picture of the very thing she needed to know.

She found it was easier, too, not to flare up and talk back. With her hand over her wallet in her pocket and the memory of the broom in her mind, she did not care really about all the jibes and jabs and having to eat a sandwich alone in the lunchroom while the next table over Ann, Esther, and even Selma giggled and cackled at the tops of their voices.

For the first time she discovered herself listening, really listening when teachers tried to explain things between the irritating squawking of the interroom communication. At library period she found herself hunting for a book in a section she had never troubled to glance at before. When the librarian came along, looking overly patient and tired, and asked was there something she wanted, Monnie surprised herself again by saying yes— did they have a book about old houses—real old houses where people used to cook in the fireplaces, before there were stoves.

There was such a book, she discovered, full of pictures. Leaning right against the wall beside the fireplace in one such picture there was a broom —a broom exactly like the one in her wallet.

She was so interested in it that she went up to the desk again and pointed out the picture to the librarian.

"How," she demanded, "could they get things clean? This broom isn't even straight across the bottom like ours."

"There were no factory-made brooms then. People made their own." Miss Ashford settled back in her chair. "There are odd stories about brooms like these. They were supposed to be made out of certain trees or bushes only—for magic reasons—"

Monnie laughed uneasily. "Like witches riding on brooms?"

Miss Ashford nodded. "Yes, that is one of the old legends. A broom made of elder wood was supposed to be a witch's horse when she rode through the night. Many times people would not allow an elder to grow near their homes. But there were other trees and plants that were good, and to use a broom made from them meant sweeping away a lot of ill luck—something our vacuum cleaners can't promise us today."

Monnie looked at the broom picture again. "Is there a book—one about the good trees and the bad ones?" she asked.

"We don't have one here—but I can order one if you are really interested." Miss Ashford, Monnie thought, suddenly, did not look quite so tired or as if she wished people would just not bother her for a while.

And, to Monnie's new sense of surprise, she found herself once more saying, "Please, I would like that. And can I take this one?"

As she packed the book of the broom into her bookbag she felt queer for a moment, as if she were not altogether Monnie Fitts any more. But of course that was not true.

That afternoon, she left the bus once more at the other stop and made her way into the dump field. There was the mailbox still upright—but the flag was down, and the lid a little open—on nothingness. Monnie squatted down beside it and tore a half-page out of her notebook. For the first time that she could remember she printed two words which had not been forced out of her because some grownup demanded that she be polite —whether she wanted to or not.

"Thank you."

Then she added so there might be no mistake:

"Monnie Fitts"

She shut the message firmly into the box, forcing up the flag as high as she could make it go.

# 3

## What Can You Do With a Wand?—Sa Boom!

Bim scuffled along, sending an empty beer can flying. He had intended to follow Monnie, just why he did not know. But she had gotten off the bus a stop early—back at Amsterdam. Which meant she had cut across the dump lot. The mailbox—the spy box! Bim hesitated. He wanted to see if there was anything in that box—if Monnie had been there. That is, in one way he did. In another, he did not want to get anywhere near it.

He kicked at another can and tried to make up his mind. There was no one around anywhere —unless someone was hiding out. He could sort of just sneak up on the box and—

"Yaaah, yaah, yaah!"

Bim jumped and then fled, all thoughts of exploring the dump lot flying out of his mind. His lunchbox banged against his legs as he ran. Matt and the gang!

His side hurt him hard by the time he reached the hall door of the project. Matt and the others were across the street, watching. He knew why, too, and it was going to be tough to keep ahead of the gang for a while. Bim rubbed the edge of his hand under his nose and sneezed. Maybe—if he could make Mrs. Johnson believe he had the flu. . . .

The trouble had all started in the hall when Matt used the water pistol. He had aimed straight at Bim and Bim had dodged, so that a stream of ink—not water—had gone right across the front of Mr. Andrew's shirt.

Bad luck for Matt—worse for Bim, because Matt had made it very plain that Bim was somehow to blame for that unlucky shot. He should just have taken it right in the face as Matt intended. Bim scowled. It was NOT his fault. Why should he stand still and let Matt squirt him all over with red ink—like he was a dummy or something?

He stamped up to the second floor step by step, getting madder inside every time he thought about it. If Matt did not hang around with Red and Pete and Hunky, he'd. . . . But Bim really knew that, with or without his gang, Matt would always have the advantage over him—unfortunately. He sniffed twice—hard and experimentally. There—that *did* sound like a cold, a real bad one.

But Mrs. Johnson was not there when he went in to try that extra special sniff on her. He could hear the slam of the fridge door out in the kitchen. However, when he hurried along to dump his lunchbox on the ledge near the sink, he discovered Monnie busy taking one doughnut out of the box while she already held another in her mouth. There was a glass of milk on the table right beside a book in which a queer purplish looking envelope was stuck for a bookmark. Monnie dropped both doughnuts beside her milk and scowled at him as if she would like to sweep him right out of the room.

"I got as much right here as you!" he snapped.

For a moment he expected a hot answer from Monnie. Instead she just looked at him for a long minute and then she got another glass from the cupboard and poured more milk.

"There're two doughnuts left," she said matter-of-factly.

Monnie's actions were so different from what Bim expected that he went around to the other side of the table cautiously, half believing she might grab back the milk, perhaps even accidentally-done-a-purpose spill it.

Instead she sat down on one of the stools and

33

finished off her first doughnut, paying him no attention, though he watched her with quick sidelong glances as he helped himself to his own after-school snack. Monnie still was not looking at him, rather at the wall straight ahead of her as if she were watching TV. Bim hesitated, doughnut in one hand, milk glass in the other.

He wanted company—not to go down the hall and just sit in his own room. He wanted someone to talk to, even if it was only Monnie, and she would probably snap his head clean off if he spoke to her.

Then, suddenly, she stopped looking at that wall and slapped open her book, holding it down flat with one hand while she licked the powdered sugar left from the doughnuts off the fingers of the other. Bim edged around a little so he could see the picture which spread clear over two pages. It showed the inside of a house with a great big fireplace—a fireplace where a pot hung on a chain over the fire.

Monnie was running her finger up and down another part of the picture—something that leaned against the wall beside that fireplace. What it was Bim could not see clearly.

Curiosity got the better of the caution he always used with Monnie. "What're you reading?"

"Not reading," Monnie denied, but she did not speak sharply. "Just looking. You ever see a broom like this?" She swept her finger well to one side and actually moved her shoulder so he could come closer for a better look.

"Broom?" Bim was completely surprised. What did Monnie want to know about a *broom*. And the one in the picture—if it *was* a broom—looked like nothing but a bunch of sticks tied to a longer pole.

"Like this one!" Now Monnie spoke with her old impatience and stabbed the bundle of sticks with the end of her finger.

"No." Bim kept on the safe side and added nothing to that.

"They used to make them just like that—when people lived in log houses." Monnie made the longest speech without any yelling at him he could ever remember. "They cut off a lot of branches of bushes and things and tied them around a big one. Miss Ashland says that these were the kind of brooms witches were supposed to ride. And there were just certain bushes or trees you could make them out of—"

"Witches." Bim settled back on the other stool with a thump. "What you talking 'bout witches for? Halloween isn't for a month yet. You going to be a witch?" He thought that might be a good choice—with all her dark hair stringing around her thin face and those big heavy eyebrows, she did look a little like a witch. Put a big wart on her nose, or something like that, and she would not even need to wear a mask.

35

Now that she was making a mean face at him again—just like her old self—well, she looked like a girl witch more than ever.

"I—oh, you wouldn't understand, you double bonehead!" Monnie slammed the book shut, put her milk glass in the sink but made no move to sweep the crumbs of her snack off the table, and marched out.

Left alone, Bim felt like himself again—for a few seconds. Then, once more, he wanted to talk to someone—only there was no one at all. He sullenly picked up his workbook, left *his* milky glass right where it was, and stamped down the hall to his room where he threw himself on his bed and lay looking up at the ceiling.

Tomorrow—tomorrow, Matt and the rest would be laying for him unless he could pretend he was sick and stay away from school. But he thought that was not going to work. Mrs. Johnson was too hard to fool. So. . . . Monnie hardly ever went to the Walker Street bus stop. She usually was already on the bus by the time it reached there. Which meant she cut across the dump lot, went down two streets, and waited at Amsterdam.

Why could he not do the same? He would not have to go with Monnie tomorrow, either. She had a dentist appointment her Miss Reeder had arranged and Mrs. Johnson would drive her in the other way to town. Once he was on the bus Matt and the others could not start anything. Mr.

Chambers was too tough to try that with—not on his bus!

His problem temporarily solved, Bim gave a small sigh of relief. He paid no attention to the workbook, but pulled out his superheroes comics and lost himself in their exploits—wondering how it would feel to be able to pull a plane right down out of the sky, stop a train with his bare hands, or just pick up Matt Pringle and the rest of the gang and drop them into a great big ditch somewhere.

You didn't really have to use just your hands, either, to be like a bionic man. There was this guy Wonder-Brain; he just thought and bang—what he thought happened! Suppose he, Bim Ross, could walk into class tomorrow and point his finger at Miss Ames and say:

"I get all A's next report time!" And—bam—that's what he would get. . . .

Reports—Bim's daydream broke on a very sharp point. Next week was half-monthly reports —they'd just started having those for the kids who could not make the grade on the big test they'd all had to take the beginning of the year. And he was sure he was not going to do very well this time, either. He reached out for the workbook and riffled the pages with no enthusiasm. What was the use? He just got all hot and cold and squirmy inside every time they even said test. Everything went out of his mind as if some superman took an eraser and went at his brains to wipe them clean.

Life sure messed a guy up. If it wasn't getting Matt really mad at him and ready to give him the works, then it was school coming down hard and heavy. A guy just couldn't win. No use even trying.

So he did not. Instead he stayed up to watch *Man Hunter* on TV until Mrs. Johnson chased him to bed. And he gave a spiteful kick to the workbook before he climbed under the covers.

And he dreamed. But this was one of the queerest dreams he had ever had. First it was so real—like it was happening. He even felt cold as if he *was* out in the night just wearing his pajamas. And he recognized where he was, too. This was the dump lot. There was the car—all bunched up like it was ready to jump at him. But right straight ahead was the mailbox—Monnie's spy box. There were spots of light down a line on its front—the second one very bright and clear.

When he looked straight at that he did not feel cold or afraid—much—any more. And when Bim awoke he seemed to remember his dream as if that spark of light still hung steadily before his eyes.

So in the morning when he did follow his plan and cut across the dump lot, having scouted from the hallway for any signs of Matt or the others, he took the path past the box.

The flag was up. Bim paused. That meant there was something inside.

But Monnie could not have left anything this morning. She was already on her way to the dentist's. Mrs. Reeder always made early appointments so you did not miss too much school. Anyway, Monnie was safely out of the way and he had a chance to see what she had put in here— maybe even to find out who was in with her on this spy thing.

Bim crouched down and caught hold of the lid of the battered box and gave a pull. It opened so easily this time he nearly lost his balance. There was a letter inside—or at least a purple envelope.

Eagerly he jerked it out. But. . . .

Written across the front in red letters—though a lot neater than any he could make—was his own name just as he had left it on the box front: "Bim Ross."

He almost threw the envelope away. Then he looked all around, moving so he could see even behind him. *They* knew him, *they* might be watching right now! He did not know who "they" might be—which made it worse.

But once more he held the envelope close to the light; that *was* his name. Now he saw the other markings—two stars up in the right hand corner, and on the left a single line of writing— "Seven Spells." Should he throw it away? Somehow he could not. Instead he tucked his find into

39

the front of his windbreaker, slammed the mailbox shut again, and started on a run for the Amsterdam corner.

He would just take it to school and there throw it into the first wastebasket. He'd rip it up, of course, so no one could read his name.

His stop in the dump had made him late and he was just in time to join at the very end of the line moving in for seats. Which put him in a front one. All to the good. When Matt and the others got on they wouldn't dare start anything here, and he might get out first and make it into school before they could grab him.

But the letter—who was writing to him—and why? To warn him against spying? He had to know.

Bim pulled out the envelope. It was not so brightly purple now and the words in the upper left corner had faded out a lot. But his name remained as plain as ever. He worked his finger under the flap and it came up easily.

Inside was a sheet of paper rolled around something. When he shook it out he saw it was a flat strip of metal—silvery colored—and about as long as his middle finger, well past the first knuckle. Along it on one side were queer marks—some looked like little faces, almost too tiny to see clearly, of animals and of men. Bim, peering at them, was uneasily glad he could *not* see them very well—some were *so* queer. On the other side

40

were squiggles as if someone had drawn queer lines, the way people do on telephone pads when they are listening to a call.

The paper which had been wrapped around it had two red words printed in large letters—letters he certainly could read:

"Sa–boom"

Whatever that meant. The bus was slowing down. There were Matt and Tony and Pete waiting all right.

Bim, without realizing just what he was doing, let the hand holding the flat metal strip move so that the end of what he held pointed directly at the door.

"Sa–boom!" Was that what he had really said?

The steady purr of the bus grew louder. They were pulling in to pick up the waiting children. He saw Mr. Chambers trying to get the door open. But in spite of all the driver could do, it remained stuck tight. Finally they started on, but the same thing happened at the next three stops, too. Mr. Chambers' neck looked red and sweaty—and the rest of the children were beginning to notice. There were questions being shouted out. Some people in the back were getting excited and one girl started to cry.

Bim gulped. He began to have a frightening feeling that what he held had something to do with the strange actions of the bus. Here they were—at the school parking lot. He almost believed that the bus would roll right by it, with them all prisoners. But no, Mr. Chambers made a mighty effort and they did pull in, but with only about two-thirds of their regular number on board.

The bus came to a stop just where it always did. Bim hurriedly wrapped up the wand thing and stuck it back into the envelope, the envelope inside his coat. The first of the kids were already jamming up by the doors. The doors opened and they spilled out—scattering fast, some of them even running.

Bim walked. With Matt and the rest left well behind he had nothing to fear. Now that he was able to look back on it all, this was an interesting adventure. Mr. Parsons who had parking lot duty was talking to Mr. Chambers now, and the latter was waving his arms around as if he were trying to explain something which he could not do easily. He climbed back into the bus and was opening and shutting the doors as if to prove that it could be done. Bim grinned and walked on into the outer hall.

He felt different today—as if things were coming all *his* way for a change. Would Mr. Chambers have to go back now and pick up the rest of the kids? If he *could*. Maybe the doors would not work again when the bus was away from the school.

But they must have because Matt and the rest did appear. They were late, of course. But they had a slip from Mr. Parsons and were told that since they had missed the beginning of the test they would have to make it up during library time.

Bim paid them little attention; he was intent on the questions before him. To his surprise he found that he could answer most of them after all. It was as if that frightening feeling, which had always made him so bone-headed when he faced an exam paper with the clock ticking away, had loosened its hold on him. It was still there, but he could fight it this time.

When he had first sat down, he had taken the purple envelope out of his shirt pocket, and now the silvery wand lay under his left hand as he wrote with his right.

He saw Miss Ames get up to give out the math part of the test.

"Sa–boom!" Bim whispered without quite realizing it.

For a moment she stared down at the sheets in her hand and then shuffled the papers back and forth as if they were out of order. After she had done that twice, she looked up at the class, a very queer expression on her face:

"There has, apparently, been a mistake made at the printing office," Miss Ames said. "We shall have to delay the rest of this test until I am sent the proper papers." She put the pack she held back on her desk with a slap as if she were definitely annoyed.

Bim passed the paper he had finished along to the front where they were being collected. Lucky —he never had been able to get that math straight in his head. At least he had a day or so more before he had to start worrying again.

The metal wand felt warmish, and he slipped it back into his pocket. Maybe it was a luck piece —he had heard about them. First the bus acting so queer and now the math papers being mixed up. . . .

One of them blew from Miss Ames's desk to the floor. Bim squinted at the test paper as he stooped down to retrieve his pencil. It was all just a lot of squiggly lines—like—like those down the back of his wand!

"Sa–boom!" he repeated in a whisper so faint even he could not hear it. What had happened? Now he felt uneasy again and not relieved. Hurriedly he jammed the wand tighter into his pocket, wanting nothing more to do with it, yet fearing to lose it. What *was* it?

# 4

Voo-Don't Doll

Monnie explored with tonguetip the new filling. It ached a little, but not much, and she would have to remember not to bite down hard there. On the credit side she had had to wait at the dentist because there had been an emergency. So by the time they were through with her, she and Mrs. Johnson had had to eat at the hamburger place on 12th Street, and it was too late to go on to school. In fact they did stop there, but it was only because it was on the way home and they could pick up Bim.

He started in talking right away and Monnie was ready to put on her bored listening face and think about something else. Except that what Bim had to say, for once, was interesting. He told

45

about the bus—how the doors wouldn't open—
so a lot of the kids were late. Then he went on
about the test and how the printers had made
some mistake.

Mrs. Johnson was frowning. "Trouble with the
bus." She shook her head. "That's not good. Maybe Henry can arrange to go a little later in the
morning and take you both in—I don't like the
idea of you riding on a bus where the doors won't
open—"

"Oh, it's all right now," Bim answered. "They
took it out again and that time everything went
okay. They tried it twice, I heard Mr. Parsons say,
and they had a mechanic go over, too, and check
on it. But it sure was queer."

Monnie noticed that he kept one hand pressed
against his chest as if he hurt inside. But he
was not even sniffing as he had yesterday. Only
now and then she was aware that he looked at
her hard, as if he wanted to say something but
could not quite do so. There was something else
about him. Usually he looked like a scared mouse
—as if he expected any moment someone was
going to hit him.

It was that look of his which often made Monnie long to do just that. He was the kind of kid
who made people feel like picking on him, always smiling a lot as if he could make you feel
better about him if he did that. Bim, she sus-
pected, spent most of his days being afraid of

things. Maybe even at night his dreams were afraid dreams, too.

Dreams. . . . She took a tighter hold of her purse. In it was the broom still wrapped in its paper. Monnie wished she had a chain so she could wear it. Maybe she could put it on a piece of string. Once around her neck under her sweater and blouse she would be sure it was safe. Monnie forgot Bim's unusual look of confidence and thought more about the broom.

Sweep clean! There was not much you could sweep away with a little broom like that. What did one sweep? Mrs. Johnson had a vacuum for the floors and a mop for the kitchen and bathroom. Monnie was well acquainted with both, since they entered into her portion of the weekly house chores from time to time, unless she could dodge doing them.

No, the silver broom was not meant to be used in any house. Where then?

Sweep clean. . . . She moved uneasily. Something had to be swept—she was sure of that. But she was not certain what, or where, or when— not yet.

They came down the dump lot street and for the first time Monnie asked a question.

"How old is this place anyway?" She wanted to ask how old was the store and the house behind it. But the house was still too much of a secret to share, or to threaten to share even by asking about it.

"Why, I don't know." Mrs. Johnson looked a little surprised. "It is one of the older sections of town. When I was a little girl we never came down here much. It was a rough place and the people who lived here—or in the buildings that used to be here—were not the kind any one on our side of town wanted to know.

"A lot of the houses were boarded up and falling apart even then. But I did hear a friend of my mother's say once that this had been the very first part of Ingleston."

"Ingleston?" Monnie repeated.

"Oh, that was the name of another town, really, one that Chesterson swallowed up when the big factory was built and so many people moved in. Chesterson before that was across the railroad and more toward the hills. But Ingleston was older. You should ask your teacher about that, Monnie—it's kind of local history, I suppose."

She turned the car into a side street to move into the project parking place.

"I wish they'd get that mess cleaned up and start on the park and recreation place they promised when we moved here. But I guess that was just a promise—a politician's promise. Help me with these bags, Bim."

Laden down with shopping bags they made their way to the apartment. Foremost in Monnie's mind was the mailbox. How soon dared she slip out to go to it? Had they—or whoever had left that message—found her note? If she left another asking about the broom and what it really meant, would "they" answer her?

She slipped into her room to find a piece of string to hang the broom from and then paused just inside the door. It was as if for the first time she really *saw*—like she had always been half-blind or something like that and now put on glasses which made everything clear.

A mess—this room was a mess.

She had spread the covers up on her bed, that was true. She would have heard from Mrs. Johnson if she had not. But the closet stood a little open and she could see shoes kicked off, even a dress lying on the floor where it had slipped from the hanger. And the top of the bureau! A lot of the things there belonged to Stella—but they were all mixed-up and powder had spilled and. . . .

For the first time Monnie *did* see and what she saw she did not like. Not liking led her to action she would never have dreamed of earlier. She set to work as if she did indeed hold a demanding broom in her hand and was about to both sweep clean and away.

She could not have told why it made her feel so much better when things looked orderly, when she had made a pile of grubby blouses and jeans to be taken to the wash, and had put shoes togeth-

49

er and wiped up the spilled powder, set all Stella's boxes and jars straight, taken her own comb and brush into the bathroom and given them a good scrub.

She looked in the mirror while she was doing that. Then made a squinty-eyed face. The Monnie Fitts she saw framed there looked as if she needed to be swept clean, also. Her straggling hair hung over her eyes, and her face—it needed washing about as much as her shirt.

By suppertime Monnie had not only made a trip to the washer-dryers in the basement, but had done as much as she could with the room—and herself. She had even spent two of her allowance quarters on the wash. And she was as tired as if she had walked about a thousand miles—or at least half a hundred.

"Sweep . . ." she said to herself, standing with her fists on her hips, staring critically about her. "I guess I did—and dusted, and washed and—"

"What happened?"

Stella had come up behind her and was gazing past Monnie's shoulder with both her eyes and mouth open.

"Don't tell me!" She closed her eyes and held one hand across them. "Just let me guess . . . Earthquake?"

Monnie, who seldom felt like laughing at any of Stella's teasing, did this time. "Wrong," she answered. She had found there was a good feeling in her, strong, if not stronger than the tiredness.

"Then you've been offered a million dollars to do this on TV and are practicing!" was Stella's prompt second guess.

"No, I guess," Monnie said slowly, "I just got tired of being so messy. I took a broom to the place—"

Stella dropped her hand from her eyes. "More than a broom, my girl. Are you sure it wasn't a shovel and a ditchdigger? And do you feel well?"

Monnie's good feeling was beginning to fade. Stella knew just the tone of voice to use to make her prickle all over.

"I cleaned up a little," she snapped. "Anything wrong about that?"

"Seeing that it is you doing it, I don't know—"

"Well, try to find out then!" Monnie pushed past the older girl. Somehow during her struggle with the cleaning she had forgotten her earlier hope of visiting the mailbox. Maybe she could go now. . . . But it was already too late. Mr. Johnson had come home and dinner was on the table. Going out after dark—that was the last thing the Johnsons were going to let her do.

She ate sullenly. All the satisfaction that had bubbled up in her during the clean-up was gone as Stella told about it. The older girl made her efforts sound like a joke. And Monnie retreated farther and farther into herself.

If she had a house, a real house of her own, like the one she had thought about for so long—that would be fun to keep neat and in order. But she never had anything but the use of part of somebody else's house and so it did not matter if she left it messy. See if she would ever clean up again!

Still, when she climbed into the upper bunk a while later, she sniffed a little. There was the smell of Stella's perfume and powder—she had gone out on a date. But there were other smells, too—like that of cleaning fluid and polish and ... Yes, if Monnie had her own house she would want it to smell just this way all the time! Once more she closed her eyes firmly so she could see somewhere inside her head that house she wanted so badly.

Only she never reached it. She could see the front door standing open ready for her to come in. But try as she would Monnie could not get to it. It was nighttime and a stream of light came from the door—just enough to show Monnie that she was—

In the dump lot!

Now something to one side sparkled—of course, the mailbox stars! She turned farther around so she could see them more clearly. One

—two—three—four—five—six—seven. All of them were glowing—but it was number three that shone the brightest. Three—why not two? Monnie tried hard now, twice as hard, to reach the box and see what it held for her this time. But then the dream broke, just as if the whole thing were a window and someone hurled a rock through it.

It was morning and Stella was pulling at her shoulder.

"Get up, kid. You sure have nothing on *your* conscience the way you can sleep! At least you can find your clothes this morning—"

"All right." Monnie squirmed over the edge of the bunk and dropped to the floor. It was odd not to land, as she usually did, on a pile of clothing she had dropped there the night before. The remains of her craving for neatness had led her to put them instead on a chair.

Stella was using a lipstick, frowning in concentration into the mirror as she stroked it on with the care of one completing a painting. Monnie drew a deep breath and then plunged:

"Stella, you remember that chain you broke— the one with the sea gull pendant on it?"

"What? Oh, that thing Ralph gave me for my birthday. Sure, I remember it—should be somewhere in my box. Why?"

"Do you want it any more? I mean, you don't

53

go with Ralph now, and you said you lost the sea gull off it. The chain—it's still broken?"

"Probably, since I never got it fixed. What do you want with it?"

"Just—well, I've got a bead-thing—we're making them in school . . ." which, Monnie told herself quickly, was no lie at all. They were making dough into beads, though the rough product of her own hands was certainly *not* worth wearing.

Stella screwed her lipstick into its case and glanced at Monnie for a moment. "Oh, all right, kid. If you can find it"—she gave a small push of the three-drawered jewel box toward the younger girl—"it's all yours."

Monnie did find it as Stella slammed out of the room. It was broken, of course, but a piece of thread could connect the links, Monnie was certain, and she could tie it in a loop around the broom. She would fix it tonight and then she would never again have to worry about losing the broom.

But the memory of her dream remained. She must hurry, be quick enough to go through the dump lot and see if the mailbox held anything. Why, it could have been there since yesterday, since she had had to go to the dentist then!

Mrs. Johnson was talking about the school bus again this morning. She had checked over the phone with Mrs. Lutz and Mrs. Rinehart, but they had decided that it must be safe today, and none of them could make up a car pool anyway. Monnie took her bookbag and her lunchbox, shouted a general " 'Bye" to the room and was gone as Bim took the first sip of his orange juice.

He was slow this morning because he had been listening to the phone conversations about the bus. Monnie had seen him grinning behind Mrs. Johnson's back as if he knew something. But Bim was going to have problems of his own. She had heard about Matt Pringle and the gang watching for him. And she did not believe that he was going to follow her, he would be far too busy looking out to make sure they were not after him.

She made a fast trip to the mailbox. Sure enough—the flag was up. Almost sick with excitement, Monnie knelt to open its door. Yes! There was another envelope—a purple envelope —inside. And this felt fatter and heavier in her hand. Her name was in the same bright red lettering as before—and she looked at the corners, too.

Seven Spells—but there were three stars in the other corner instead of one. Maybe they *were* stamps and three were needed to carry a heavier envelope.

Monnie could not wait to open it—or at least peek. No waiting this time until she was on the bus. And the contents *were* very different, even though she had not really expected another broom.

This was a doll, made flat like a paper doll. She was dressed in a smart jeans suit—and the jacket of it could be taken off. But the oddest thing about her was her head. It was cut in the shape of a head right enough, a head with a lot of longish hair. But it was mirror bright and had no paint at all on the face or the hair, as if—an odd thought crossed Monnie's mind—it was unfinished and left for her to do.

With the doll were tiny loose flowers, all glittery, shining like diamonds, or rubies. And each flower formed the head of a pin. Wrapped around the pins and the doll with no face or hair was a sheet of paper.

"Voo-don't. Use with a good heart."

"Voo-don't?" Monnie repeated. It sounded a little like something she had heard, or read. Voo-don't—Voodoo! That silly rag doll Selma had brought to school when she said Miss Ames ought to get a headache so they wouldn't have her for study hall when Selma wanted to sneak out early and go downtown to get tickets for the big performance of the Swooners. She had laid the doll down and stuck a pin right through its head.

Only it had not worked. Miss Ames had been right there on duty and Selma never got her tickets. She had been mad and thrown the doll in the wastebasket when the period was over. That had been a voodoo doll—one to hurt people. But what in the world was a Voo-don't one?

Filled with curiosity Monnie stuck her new prize in her wallet and ran down the street. If she missed the bus there would have to be a lot of explanations and she could not think of one that might honestly sound like the truth.

She was not aware that Bim had followed her until he caught up with her just before they reached the bus stop.

"What did you find?" he demanded breathlessly. "What did you get—out of that old mailbox!"

Monnie held her wallet all the tighter. So she had been right—he was spying on her! It was a good thing she had reached the box first or she might never have found her own personal envelope.

"None of your business!" she said loudly and pushed in among the waiting girls just as the bus pulled up to the curb. At least the doors opened easily this morning though she saw Mr. Chambers watching them carefully. She went back to the middle, plumping herself down beside Alice Paxton before Ruth Ritche could reach the seat. Both girls glared at her and Alice pushed over as if to dump Monnie out in the aisle. But Monnie just stiffened and held on. This morning she hardly noticed anyone around her. Her mind was fully taken up by only two thoughts. One that Bim was, and would be, spying on her perhaps every time she visited the mailbox, a belief that brought such a frown of anger to her face that Alice stopped her quiet shoving and drew back to her own side of the seat.

The second thought was gaining in importance. What was a Voo-don't doll and how was she to use it? For that it was to be used in some manner Monnie had no doubts at all.

# 5

## A Light for the Dark

Monnie slid the Voo-don't doll from between the pages of her book and examined it more carefully in the light. If it were not for the blank and shiny head it would certainly look like—well, almost like Stella when she was all dressed up in her new suit ready for a date.

No, maybe not Stella. . . . Monnie blinked. It almost seemed as if under her very eye the doll had grown shorter, a little thicker of body—more like Selma even. She shot a glance over the edge of her book to where Selma lounged in her seat, one hand twisting in her long hair, the other tapping with her finger on the edge of her desk as if she were keeping time to music she could hear even if no one else did. Selma—huh!

Then there was Ann Perry—and Esther. . . .
Monnie surveyed the two rows before her, sin-
gling out each girl. However, for some reason, her
eyes kept coming back to Selma. For the first
time she wondered what it would be like to be
Selma—or, say, Alice Paxton. What if something
queer might happen some morning and everybody
suddenly changed bodies. Would they still be
themselves in a different body—or. . . .

Monnie had never thought anything like that
before. It was strange. She looked back down at
the doll and was so startled that she nearly let out
a sound. The head of the doll was no longer blank
and shiny. It was Selma, just as if it was a very
clear photograph of her and she was lying there
looking back up at Monnie questioningly. As if
she wanted something. . . . What?

Selma was nothing to Monnie but a girl to be
avoided, with all her everlasting talk about the
Swooners and the Prancers—or whatever group
of singers was in favor right then. Monnie took
her finger and tried to rub away the pictured face
on the doll. It did not go. She glared down at it
now—if it was going to be Selma, she did not
want it! That was for sure.

But the longer she looked at the doll's head,
the more that odd feeling in her battled with her
impatience and dislike. Selma was no friend. She
looked stupid with her little squinty eyes and her

mouth nearly always open even when she was not talking.

There was a sharp prick in Monnie's finger, the very one she had used to rub away that face. She had put it down on one of the flower-headed, very short pins that had come with the doll. And the pin stuck to her so she did not shake it free at once.

The pin had a head like a very tiny rose of a deep red. Monnie picked it loose from her finger, but she continued to hold it.

Voo-don't doll—and the one Selma had brought to school and stuck pins in. Voodoo— Voo-don't. . . . Monnie repeated both words in her mind. Selma had wanted to hurt when she had used that other doll. Some of the girls had half-believed she could do it. Only it had not worked. How could sticking pins in a doll cause anyone to have a headache?

The rose pin—it was pretty. Just as . . . well, Selma would look better, wouldn't she, if she'd just stop twisting her hair and sometimes close her mouth tight and keep it that way. Monnie's hand moved. She found herself inserting the rose pin into what was a very tiny hole in the doll's head, as if the flower pin had been set just like that to keep some of those long strings of hair in place. And once there, the flower stuck.

"Monnie?"

She started and clapped her book flat down on the doll.

"Yes, Miss Ames?"

"Do you have your project selected for Friday after next?"

Project—what project? Monnie's thoughts could not be sorted out so quickly. Then she remembered the visit to the library—which now seemed to have happened about a hundred years ago—and the book about the old houses. She did not know what her project was really going to be, but she could bluff that right now.

"Yes, Miss Ames," she answered with what she hoped would be taken for complete confidence.

She thought Miss Ames did not share that confidence. Too often in the past Monnie's project efforts had been complete failures or as near to that as made no matter. Monnie was not good with her hands, and to make a box scene, or do a poster, or worse, write a poem or a one-page story was a task beyond her. She could think of what she wanted to say—but it never came out right on paper. So lately she had given up even trying to get that much done.

Now she waited until Miss Ames had turned her back and was writing on the board to sneak another peek at the doll. It was blank—and the flower pin had fallen out. Monnie glanced at Selma. The other girl was sitting up straighter—

62

and somehow . . . she looked. . . . Monnie shook her head. This was just imagining things.

But twice more that day she consulted the doll. Once it put on Miss Ames' face and then she gave it a white row of little tiny flowers for a kind of crown. Right after that Miss Ames lost the frown that always made her look so cross and demanding, and she actually laughed at something one of the boys had said.

The last time Monnie studied the doll she had thought of Stella for some reason and this time, with deliberation, she chose a yellow flower and put it not in the head of the doll, but instead in a hole at the throat. Stella, for all her teasing, could be nice—she had given Monnie the chain and. . . .

Someone paused beside her desk just as she put the doll into her wallet. "What you doing Saturday after next?"

Monnie was startled. Selma stood there.

"Why?" The first thing that came to her was that question.

Selma started to twist a piece of hair around in her fingers and then loosed it. She looked a little bewildered as if she did not know the answer to such a question.

"Well—we're going over to Alice's—she got two new albums—Beenie Schultz and his Block Busters. Want to come along?"

Monnie's gape grew wider. It was the first time

since she had come to the Johnsons' that such an invitation had been given to her.

"We're going to talk about the Halloween thing, too," Selma continued, "you know—what we're going to wear and all at the party."

The Halloween party, Monnie had learned through the past few weeks at Langley, was a very exciting event. But until this moment she had had no idea of being a part of it.

"You coming?" Selma demanded, some of the old whining note back in her voice as if whatever had moved her to speak to Monnie was already wearing off.

"Maybe, if I can. . . ." Monnie found herself answering. But Selma had already turned away.

Monnie sat very still for a long moment, but her thoughts were busy. You stuck pins in a voodoo doll to hurt. What happened with a Voodon't doll? Did it mean that the flowered pins she used in her gift from Seven Spells were meant to act in directly the opposite fashion? There would be no harm in trying to see if that was the truth.

Though she did not take out the doll again to look at it, she thought of Stella—hard—and wished for her something nice—even though she was not sure what would be "nice" as far as Stella was concerned. Maybe a raise in pay or even a new boyfriend—Monnie didn't think much of Fred who came around now—but something good.

She hardly saw the other children on the bus as she climbed in. She would just have to wait and see—would something good happen to Stella? And if it did—Monnie took a long breath—what did she have here? And how could she use it? A Voo-don't doll—why, she could maybe make all sorts of things happen to people! If it would only work!

Bim slouched down in the seat. He had made it through the day anyway. Mr. Parsons had his eye on Matt and the rest—they had not been able to corner him. Luckily Matt had had to stay after school this time. The ink gun was still hanging over his head. And without Matt maybe the rest would let Bim alone. He put one hand inside his jacket and found the strip of metal with those queer letters on it. No more Sa-boom—he was afraid of trying it again now. But had it really and truly locked the bus doors? He wished he dared prove it true.

Anyway they had not gotten the new test papers back yet so he had not had to worry about math today. He saw Monnie up ahead. She was sitting there very quietly, staring out of the window so intently that he turned his head to look too. It was as if there was something very important to be seen there. But that was not true—just the same old streets.

Was she going to get off at Amsterdam? The

mailbox—something waiting there for her. No, she had gotten up for their own street stop.

Bim watched her leave and she never looked around at all. Waiting until the next stop, he ducked out the door. Then he watched the junk lot cautiously, expecting to see her come in from the other side, but there was no sign of Monnie. Bim scuffed on into the junk lot toward the mailbox. Maybe there wouldn't be anything today—or if there had been Monnie had already taken it. She sure had hurried out of the house that morning.

The mailbox—Bim squatted down before it. The flag was down and when he tried to open it the lid was so tight again that he could not move it. Yet it had opened easily enough before. And his name and Monnie's looked very bright and clear—just as if they had been painted on that very day. He brought out the length of metal on sudden impulse and pointed it at the box.

"Sa—boom!" he said it, not very loud but with a lot of force.

But the box remained closed against all his tugging and for some moments he wondered if he had locked it forever—or at least for some time just as the bus doors had been. Nursing that unhappy thought he went on home.

There was a visitor with Mrs. Johnson. Bim hearing that only-too-familiar voice from the hallway, made a face. He would like to have melted back out through the door again, but knew better than to try that. But what was Miss Valasco doing here today? It wasn't her usual visit time.

She came to check up on him once a month, sure. But she had been here only two weeks ago, and then he had to try to explain about the exam and she had talked about special tutoring. Maybe that was what they were planning now—more school. Bim stuck out his lower lip and wanted to kick the door hard, but knew that he did not dare.

"Bim—that you?" Leave it to Mrs. Johnson—she had ears like the radar they talked about—as well as eyes in the back of her head . . . sometimes.

"Yeah."

"Come in then."

With the utmost reluctance he did that. Miss Valasco was sitting there and she turned on that smile which he had never believed was any more real inside than the mustache Matt pasted on his upper lip when he was playing boss.

"It's good to see you, Bim."

"Hello, Miss Valasco," he answered, knowing well what was expected of him and then added quickly: "They haven't given all the repeat tests yet—there was something wrong with the papers. I don't take the math one until next week."

"And I'm sure you're going to make it this time," she assured him. "You've got a better chance at doing well than you let yourself believe. Thumbs up!" She held out her hand with the thumb up all right—though Bim did not see what all that meant.

But she did not ask him any questions. Instead she said to Mrs. Johnson, "Nothing is settled, of course. But you will be hearing from us. And good luck, Bim."

This time her smile did not look quite as put on as usual—but as if she really meant it. Then she went out, Mrs. Johnson going to the door with her, while Bim made his way to the kitchen.

Monnie was there before him again. She had a glass of milk standing by her hand and a paper napkin with two brownies on it, but she was neither eating nor drinking. Instead she had that same queer stare in her eyes.

". . . new dress . . ." she said as if Bim were not right there before her. "That's it—maybe a new dress!"

"Who's going to give you one?" Bim demanded.

Monnie actually jumped. It was as if she had not known he was there until he asked her that. Then she shook her head.

"Nobody's going to give me a dress—just maybe I'm going to give one to somebody else."

"Where would you get the money?" he asked.

She had crammed the whole of a brownie into her mouth and had to swallow twice before she answered, "I don't know—maybe I will and maybe I won't! Your Miss Valasco was here. Did she come to see how dumb you were again?"

Bim bristled. "No, she didn't! And she just wished me luck. I don't know why she came."

"Maybe she's going to move you." Monnie took a deep gulp of milk to wash down the last of the brownie. "You'll be glad to get away from Matt, won't you, if that's true?"

Be moved again? Bim glanced around the kitchen. Much as he feared Matt and the gang, and all the things he did not like about the Johnsons—there was more, he suddenly realized, that he did like or at least that seemed good here. Suddenly he did not want any after-school snack, his stomach hurt, and he hated Monnie so much for suggesting what she had that he could have slapped her face. Only he knew that if he tried that it would just end in a fight and he'd be in more trouble again. If they were only *thinking* of moving him, a fight with Monnie might make them decide to really be serious about that.

"You hear something?" he asked even though he hated to let Monnie know that she had made any impression on him. But if she had heard something, then he had to find out.

"No. Only it wasn't her day, was it? And when your social worker comes around like that it means moving—always does." Monnie nodded her head as if she had been through such a like experience so many times that she could guess at once. For a moment or two Bim thought about that. Monnie had been moved around a lot—he knew that. More than he had really, so she ought to know the signs.

Now he did not try to answer her but went to his room and sat on his bed. "His" room, "his" bed—but they were not, they belonged to the Johnsons. He did not really have any place of his own. How long would he even be here now?

He watched the Johnsons for most of the evening off and on, trying to guess something from what they said or didn't say about what might be ahead. But it seemed that everything was just as usual—though Stella came home all excited because she had been made an assistant cashier at the restaurant, and there was a chance of a raise in a couple of weeks if she made good. One queer thing—when Stella kept talking about that Monnie just sat there smiling, and it was an odd smile, one which Bim could not quite understand. He had seen Monnie smile like that only twice before and both times it was when she had put something over on someone. But what could Monnie have to do with Stella getting a promotion at work?

Bim went miserably to bed. Nobody had said anything, had even hinted that he was going to be moved. Surely they were not just going to wait until the last minute. . . . Maybe it was because he had done so badly at school. If he could pass the math exam they would change their minds. Fumbling he got out the metal strip and held it tightly in his hand.

"Sa—boom," he whispered through the dark. "Sa—boom!"

It *was* very dark, and cold. He—he was in the dump lot once more, and there was the mailbox with its glowing stars. The fear that had been in him since Monnie had talked of moving was suddenly gone. Instead he was excited, just as if this were Christmas and he had a great big box to open. The fourth star on the front of the box blazed as bright as any light on a Christmas tree. Something was in there for him—he had only to open the lid and take it out—something wonderful!

But before he could raise his hand to do just that, the dark was gone and he was back in bed. The metal wand was still in his hand. It was very early—just gray light outside. Bim wriggled out of bed and dressed as if out to win some kind of a speed record. Then, having stowed his first gift closely under his jacket, he slipped the door bolts, turned the lock, and ran down the stairs. No waiting this morning—he had to see what was at the dump lot—he had to!

There was just the first touch of red sun in the sky as he came around the wrecked car. Yes, the flag was up again! He had been so sure it would be—so very sure. Now he threw himself down and tugged at the lid.

There was no letter in there this time—rather a round package. But it had his name on it. And there were four star stamps. Bim tore anxiously at the paper. What fell out was a tube of silver— the color of the stars.

Near one end there was a button set in the side—and the tip close to that was pointed in an odd way. When he held it up so that that point was at the top it looked exactly like a lighted candle! Without thinking just what he was doing Bim pushed the button. The whole of the pointed part lit up with a blue light.

It did not spread far like the light of a flashlight. In fact it did not seem to show up except when you looked directly at it. Bim touched his fingertip to the point with great caution. No, it was not hot.

But when he chanced to hold it closer to the mailbox he saw that the fourth star on the cover of the box glimmered and turned brighter—even a little blue—as if it drew strength from this queer candle.

Pressing the button again Bim saw the light vanish. He put his treasure away as safely as he could and started back toward the apartment, running, and hoping that he had not been missed and that his early morning adventure would not be discovered.

What the light was for he could not guess, but he was sure that it would prove to be important.

# 6

---

## *Who's Afraid?*

Bim sat on the edge of his bed. He had made it back in good time. There came the burr of the electric razor from next door where Mr. Johnson was shaving, and he could smell coffee from the kitchen. But no one had been aware he had slipped out and in again. He wondered about Monnie. The envelope had *his* name on it. Now he took out the candlelike torch and tried to push the button. There was only a very small flicker of light at the pointed end and he could not press the button itself very far. But the burr of the razor stopped and he heard an exclamation from the kitchen.

At the same time the light in the hall flickered, then caught on and burned steadily again. Once more Bim tried a cautious experiment—pressing the button. The light flickered—it really did—just as the candle sparked! He could not understand what had happened or why. But he laid the most recent gift from Seven Spells down beside the Sa-boom wand and studied them both.

In spite of everything he was convinced that "Sa-boom" and the piece of metal with all its strange markings and pictures had had something to do with both the queer way the bus had acted and the messing up of the test papers. Now this candle-thing. . . .

Bim half put out his hand to try pushing the button just once more and then jerked back and away from it. Who left the purple envelopes in the mailbox? And why?

"You call Stevens," he heard Mr. Johnson saying. "There's definitely something wrong with the current. If there's a defective fuse, it's his business to see that's replaced."

Bim grabbed at the candle and the Sa-boom wand and stuffed them away. Suppose—just suppose—the candle did make lights go off, and the Johnsons found out what he had done? Who was going to believe any story about the mailbox and the things sent by Seven Spells? He shuffled quickly through his bookbag, looking for the envelopes. There was the first one, but the color was all faded away. You could not see either the name in the corner or the stars that were like stamps any more. Even his own name was now so dim it was hard to make it out. The envelope that had been wrapped around the candle was a lot paler, too.

He thought of talking to Monnie. What had she gotten out of the mailbox? Because he was sure that she had gotten something. She must know who Seven Spells were and why *he* had gotten what he had. Yes, he must corner Monnie and demand answers!

That determination sent Bim to the kitchen, to gulp down breakfast—though Mrs. Johnson warned him twice about eating so fast. But she was more worried about the electricity because she had promised to bake cookies for the church bazaar and she did not know whether the stove would work. So Bim, usually a slow eater, and reluctant to leave the apartment, was out first that morning, while Monnie went back to her room for something.

He let her get past him while he stepped back in the lower hall. And, for the first time since Matt had been laying for him, he paid no attention to the street outside, but took off after Monnie, who was going, just as he thought she would, through the junk lot.

Monnie was down on her knees pulling at the lid of the mailbox when he caught up with her.

"There's nothing there!"

She nearly threw herself off-balance she turned

so quickly, her face reddening, and her eyes sparking. Monnie was working herself up for a real fight. In spite of himself Bim drew back.

"Look here." He spoke quickly—not that he was afraid to tangle with Monnie, especially out here where the Johnsons could not witness any fighting and give him another black mark. "What's with this mailbox anyway? Who uses it —besides you? Who are Seven Spells?"

Monnie got to her feet, advanced toward him with a fierce expression on her face.

"What do you know about *them?*" she demanded in return.

"Just that they leave letters here—letters with things in them—"

"You took some?" She was madder now than he had ever seen her.

"They had my name on 'em," he countered. "Just like my name's on that box. Look!" He pulled out the two envelopes he had stuck into his pocket and waved them in her face.

Monnie grabbed—and the top envelope tore when Bim did not let go quickly enough. But you could still see his name—even Monnie must admit that.

"I found 'em in that." He pointed to the mailbox. "And they were for me. You can read the name, can't you?"

Monnie's scowl did not change but at last she nodded, very reluctantly.

78

Bim gave an inward sigh of relief. He was not afraid of Monnie now, and he did want some answers. After all, the mailbox had been her idea in the first place.

"Who's Seven Spells?" he asked again.

Monnie shrugged. "I don't know."

"But you fixed up this box, painted your name on it, you must have been waiting for them," Bim pointed out.

Monnie aimed a kick at the mailbox. "I was just thinking about letters—I never thought any would really come." She hated to admit that to Bim. In fact her one wish now was to run away —to refuse to listen to him or stay near the box. But what *had* Bim gotten in those faded envelopes? The need to know was so strong that it kept her right where she was.

"What did you get?" she asked abruptly.

For a long minute she thought Bim was not going to answer and she grew hot inside, wanting to slap him good for spoiling it all. Then she saw him take a package wrapped in a torn notebook sheet out of the front of his windbreaker.

"I got this first"—he held up the Sa-boom wand—"and this here was in there this morning." Now he displayed the candle-torch. "What did you get?" For he was sure that if he had these, Monnie, too, had received things.

"I got a broom and a doll," she answered with all of her usual sharpness.

79

A broom? Bim looked at the mailbox. Surely no broom could have been fitted into that! Monnie must be making that up.

Some impulse made her pull the broom out from under her jumper where it had hung in hiding on the mended chain. "See?"

"That's a broom?"

"It's made like one of the old time ones." Now that she had shown it—in spite of her wish—she might as well explain. "And the doll's a Voo-don't."

To Bim nothing made sense. A funny looking silver broom—even if Monnie claimed that was what it was, it did not look like that to him—and a doll! What was a Voo-don't doll? He had never heard of anything like it before.

Monnie no longer looked so mad, more as if she were thinking. Now she crouched down again and touched the front of the mailbox where there was the line of silver stars.

When she spoke she did not look up at Bim at all but kept on studying the stars.

"What are they all for?"

Bim guessed she meant the things they had found there. He hesitated. Should he tell about the bus and the exam papers and what he thought had happened as the result of his wishing and "Sa–boom"?

"What are yours for?" he countered.

"I don't know—not really." Monnie fingered

the broom where it hung around her neck. She had not shown him the doll. "At least—I'm not sure. The broom—there was a note with it that said 'Sweep clean.'"

"Sweep what?" Bim wanted to know as she paused.

"I guess . . . oh, I'm not sure."

This was a different Monnie than he had ever seen before. She had lost the frowning look she always wore, which made you sure she was going to burst out in a fight if you gave her a chance.

"The doll—it works. . . ." She sounded more certain about that.

"Works how?"

"You know about that voodoo doll Selma was showing around—the kind you stick pins into so people will get a headache or a stomachache or something?"

Bim nodded. He had heard about Selma's attempt to use it and the failure of it. Most of the fifth grade knew that story.

"Well, the Voo-don't acts just the opposite. You stick in a flower pin and wish something nice for a person—and it happens!"

Bim laughed nervously. Monnie sounded so sure that he could almost believe her. But this was part of some trick of hers, of that he was sure.

"It does!" She glared up at him with a flashing return of her old anger. "I tried it—yesterday. I

81

tried it for Stella—and it worked! She got this new job. And this morning I tried it for Mrs. Johnson —I wished her a new dress . . ."

"And I suppose she found it hanging in the closet—just like that?"

"It'll come, you'll see." Monnie nodded with confidence, and Bim was now sure that she was not playing any game with him, that Monnie really believed in her Voo-don't doll. But already she had asked a question in return.

"What do these do?" She pointed to the wand and the candle he still held in full view.

Bim hesitated. Just as Monnie seemed to be sure about the power of her Voo-don't doll, so was he certain in his own mind about the Sa-boom, as he privately thought of it now. So he took the plunge and told about the school bus and the test papers, expecting Monnie to laugh.

Instead she looked interested and as if she believed him.

"The bus was all right when they tested it later," she said. "And it's been all right ever since. I heard Miss Lewis and Miss Ames talking about those test papers—so it's true they were all mixed-up. Have you tried anything else?"

"No," Bim admitted. But he did tell her about how queerly the electricity had acted this morning when he had turned on the candle.

"Mrs. Johnson thought it was the fuses," Monnie said. "Even the stove went off for a minute and the fridge. But what's the good of something that can turn things off?"

"I don't know," Bim admitted frankly. He rolled the candle and the Sa-boom back in the paper and put them away.

Monnie picked up her bookbag. "We'd better get going. The bus'll be here soon."

Then, as they had never done before since they had both come to the Johnsons', the two started off together, not quarreling, but rather occupied with some very new thoughts.

"I think I know where the mailbox came from." Monnie broke the silence between them at last, just before they reached the bus stop.

"Where?" Bim was quick to ask.

"From the old house. I . . ."

But she had no time to add to that for the bus arrived and they both had to run for it. Inside Bim squeezed in beside a smaller boy he did not know, and Monnie sat down beside Selma who, to Monnie's surprise, moved over to make a few inches more room.

"Did you ask about going?" was her greeting.

Going—where? Monnie's mind was so full of the mailbox, of Bim's find there and her own, that she could not remember what Selma meant.

"Well, did you?" Some of the old whiny impatience was back in Selma's voice. But this morning her hair looked neater, and though she raised her hand now and then as if to twist a strand, she did not complete that old gesture.

"Not yet . . . I didn't get a chance," Monnie answered. That had really been true enough. Stella had been so full of her good luck that Monnie had not had any time with Mrs. Johnson yesterday. "I'll ask tonight—"

"Are they strict with you—the Johnsons?" Selma wanted to know. "How do you like living with them?"

Monnie had learned long ago how to answer any question about the various foster homes she had known.

"They're all right. Nice people." Then, to her amazement, she realized that this time it **was** the truth. The Johnsons *had* been nice to her. In spite of all Miss Reeder, her social worker, could and must have told them about how she had never seemed to fit in well any place, they had never mentioned that. Stella, in spite of her teasing, was not too bad. She had given Monnie the chain without asking anything in return for it. And Mrs. Johnson—well, for a foster lady, she had not been too bad at all. The Johnsons, Monnie decided suddenly, were really about the best foster guardians she had had—so far.

"But you have to be real careful about what you do," Selma continued. "Aren't you afraid they'll send you back?"

"Back? Where?" Monnie's hand tightened on

her wallet in which lay the Voo-don't doll. Just now she wished it was one of the other kind and she could make it work bad instead of good. "What do you mean?"

Selma screwed up her mouth and squinted her eyes. "Wherever you came from."

Monnie thought of the Lewises, which had been her last stop. No, she wouldn't be going back there. They already had taken another girl. But what if what Selma hinted at was true, that she could be moving on! In spite of the heat in the bus she felt a cold lump in her middle, as if her breakfast had suddenly turned into ice and rested there heavily.

"I'm not going anywhere," she said flatly. It would be two weeks before Miss Reeder came to make her usual visit, and Monnie could not remember now any really black mark against her. She thought of the cleaning up the broom had led her to do. She would keep on doing that and minding all she could to keep out of trouble. She would just have to be extra careful.

"Not even to Alice's?" Selma persisted with a tight smile. Then Monnie remembered the invitation from yesterday.

"I don't know—I'll ask."

After all, Alice had not asked her—that was all Selma's doing. So she could not even be sure that the invitation was a real one.

But once they were going into their room Alice did match step with her. "You coming Saturday after next?"

"I have to ask," Monnie explained. She was not sure whether she wanted to go or not. To be invited to Alice's house might mean that she could be one of the group—but she did not feel comfortable about it somehow. Then she forgot the whole question as she opened her notebook and began to read over the things she had copied out of the library book with the broom picture. There had been a lot about how the early settlers had lived and how they made almost everything in their houses with their own hands—the brooms, too. She patted her chest with her other hand and thought she felt a faint warmth there as if the broom on the chain answered her.

Bim wriggled in his seat. He had thought all the way to school about Monnie's cut-off sentences. What had she meant by "the house"? What house? That old one she went to behind the wrecked store? There were just apartments around the project, no other houses. He was so interested in his own thoughts that he was startled when Miss Ames called on him, only half hearing the question. But what he did hear gave him a clue:

"Electricity," he answered as if someone else had put the word right into his mouth.

"That's right. Now if you will just pull down the shades, Arthur, we'll see the film. . . ."

The room passed quickly into a dusky, shadowy darkness. Bim heard rustlings and movement around him and knew that Matt's gang had been alerted. Though Miss Ames had broken up their grouping and seated them all as far as possible from each other, it did not help much when they were determined on something and had a good opportunity like a film to cover it.

Out of the dark a hand grabbed Bim's arm. He jerked back and smashed into another body. Somebody cried out and there was a flash. He heard a scream—that must be from Marie in the next seat over. There was a spitting of sparks along the floor.

Without thinking, Bim closed his other hand, which was still free, on the paper in his pocket. Even through the covering, his thumb felt the knob on the side of the candle tube, and he pressed down—hard.

The spitting stopped. At the same time the blinds over the windows all cracked upward at once, letting full sunlight back into the room. Matt stood clutching Bim, his mouth open in complete surprise. Then he dropped his hold and jumped away, but not before Miss Ames bore down upon them. Bim, still in his seat, waited for the storm to break. This was all he needed, to be sent down to the principal, maybe have Mrs. Johnson called—and . . . He tried not to think of Miss Valasco's unusual visit and what that might mean for his future.

"I have had enough of this!" Miss Ames' voice was as sharp as a TV pistol shot. "Just what is going on here?" Matt's seat was an aisle away. Bill Hudson, who had moved in on Bim, was also out of place.

"Matt, you and Bill will report to Mr. Haynes immediately. You may have caused serious damage to the equipment." She glanced down at the floor where an electric cord lay in coils. The sparks had come from it, and Bim could smell burning. But there was no sign of fire.

He saw Miss Ames glance at the windows as if puzzled. But she made no comment as she assigned the rest of the class a section to read in their texts and marched off with Matt and Bill.

Bim drew a deep breath. Why had she not included him in the trouble? Perhaps it was because he had still been in his seat. Or perhaps— just perhaps, there was another reason. He slid his hand inside his jacket again to touch the package of tube and wand.

Who's afraid, he asked himself, knowing well the answer which he dared not admit. Bim Ross was—for one. What had happened ever since he had written his name defiantly on the mailbox

88

was too queer, too far removed from life as it had always been for him, to accept easily. He wanted desperately to get to Monnie again—to find out all she knew—to learn from her whether he must throw away what Seven Spells had sent him in order to be safe.

# 7

## Mirror, Mirror . . .

At least there was no school tomorrow—it was a teacher-meeting day. Bim sighed with relief, but he put his math book into his bag. That exam would be given Monday and he *had* to pass this time. Though Matt and Bill had come back from the office looking mad, they made no move toward him as he hurried for the bus. He wanted very much to get to Monnie, to learn whatever else she knew. That house she had mentioned. . . .

Monnie had heard about the trouble with the projector and that Matt seemed to have started it all. Trying to get at Bim, she thought. Had it been the candle that had stopped him?

She saw Bim get on the bus and look around for her. But she met his gaze with a blank stare.

The fact that he had two gifts from the mailbox still made her mad. That had been her own private game until he had put his name on it, too. He had no right, no right at all.

Deliberately she stayed on the bus, rode past the Amsterdam stop and got off at the corner of her own street. She had wanted to go to see the old house again, but not with Bim tagging along. In fact she must have been crazy to mention it to him at all.

Now she walked fast, knowing that Bim would do nothing to catch up with her while the other boys could see him. And she was in the hall of the apartment before he slammed in behind.

"Hey, I want to—" he began breathlessly. Monnie turned her head and gave him her best glare.

"Want then," she told him fiercely. "I'm not telling you anything at all—you understand—anything!"

She said that hardly above a whisper since there was someone in the living room talking with Mrs. Johnson and she certainly was not going to answer any more questions—from Bim, or anyone else!

Bim reached out and tried to catch her arm, but she jerked loose.

"That old house—you said something about the mailbox belonging—"

"Shut up!" she hissed just as Mrs. Johnson's voice rose louder.

"Is that you, Monnie? Please come in."

Monnie made the worst face she could twist her eyes and mouth into, and left Bim with his mouth half-open as she slouched on into the other room.

Miss Reeder sat there. She had a cup in her hand. Mrs. Johnson always had tea and cookies when the social workers came. Now both of them smiled at Monnie. It was not Miss Reeder's day at all! Why then. . . . Monnie drew a deep breath. Did her coming mean another move?

"Hello, Miss Reeder." She tried not to let anyone think it bothered her, even if there *was* going to be a move.

And she was careful not to ask questions, only give the proper answers to the ones Miss Reeder asked after Mrs. Johnson excused herself and went to pack cookies in a box to take to the bazaar. Monnie nibbled on one she had been offered, but there was no taste to it in her dry mouth. Swallowing it was like swallowing lumps of stone.

Yes, she liked school—yes, she was getting along all right, yes, and yes. . . .

If they moved her now, she would never know about the mailbox—find out about Seven Spells. Bim would have the secret all to himself. She could hardly bear to think of that happening.

"I am glad that things are going so well." Miss Reeder's smile must be getting worn out, she had kept it glued in place so long. The question Monnie wanted to ask, and yet shrank from doing, was so much on her mind that she was afraid it would come out of its own accord.

Why was Miss Reeder here at all?

But Monnie dared not ask, and it would seem that Miss Reeder had no reason for explaining. She said goodbye to Mrs. Johnson and left Monnie uneasy and more than a little afraid. Yesterday Miss Valasco had been here about Bim—today Miss Reeder.

Monnie eyed Mrs. Johnson uneasily. Were the Johnsons the ones who wanted a change? They had talked at night a lot since a letter had come last week. Monnie remembered hearing just the rumble of voices as she played her own house game. She choked on the last crumbs of the cooky she had taken and scuttled to her room. Or rather Stella's room, which she had been allowed to share.

Once inside, Monnie shut the door carefully behind her and looked around. It was in better order—yes. Ever since she had had the broom (now she raised her hand to make sure it still hung safely around her neck), she had picked up her things and tried to remember to keep them neat. But there were all those weeks before. And there were other times when she had definitely not followed the Johnsons' rules just because she was not going to have anyone tell her, Monnie Fitts, what she could or could not do.

She sat down on Stella's bed. It was almost as if she could not keep on standing there, remembering everything Mrs. Johnson might say if she had decided that Monnie was too difficult to keep. She had heard it all before too many times at other "homes."

Now with the empty feeling in her she listed all the complaints she could remember. In the past she had not cared. Being "difficult" had always made her sure she was herself—Monnie Fitts—and not just another foster child. Now—now, she did care. Oh, maybe the Johnsons were not so wonderful, but she was just tired of being moved around as if she were a doll or something to be put here and put there without any feelings of her own at all.

Doll. . . . She felt inside her jacket for her wallet and brought out the Voo-don't doll. For the first time she looked down at the blank, shiny face on it and tried to see herself there. Maybe she could wish something good just for herself. But the face remained blank.

No—there was a change coming over it!

Monnie hung over the doll where it lay on the cover of Stella's bed, watching the misty outline of a face form over the shine of the metal. But this was no face that she knew. And it was an old face. There were wrinkles around the eyes, which

95

seemed to be far back in the head as if they were almost hidden from view, though deep in those hollows she believed she could see tiny specks of blue light.

There were wrinkles around the mouth, too, drawing lines down the chin. And the skin was not pink but dull white. The hair above the high, seamed forehead was white, too, and pulled tightly back.

Who was it? There was old Mrs. Pritchett who lived down the hall. She was about the oldest person Monnie knew. But this was not Mrs. Pritchett. Though . . . the face was alive, alive in a way that the other mirror faces which had come there had never been.

Those deep-set eyes—they looked right into her in a queer fashion that was the most frightening thing Monnie had ever known. But. . . . It *had* been frightening—just at first—but now she had another feeling, a feeling that something very important was about to happen.

Monnie leaned closer to the doll face. She kept her voice to the lowest of whispers.

"Who are you? What *is* going to happen?"

She was sure she saw the lips of the face move, as if they were shaping words. But she could hear nothing, even though she nearly laid her head on top of the doll's. Then the face was gone, as if wiped away with one sweep of her finger, though Monnie's hand had never moved at all!

Quickly she slipped the doll back into its envelope and the envelope into her wallet. Then she reached up and tucked it under the pillow of her own bed. All at once she did not want to have it any closer to her.

But who had that old woman been and what had she wanted of Monnie? Because Monnie was sure there had been some important message given that she had not been able to hear. Guessing that, she was hot with her old impatience.

Then Mrs. Johnson called from the kitchen and Monnie, having shed her jacket, went quickly to answer. The other nagging fear had come back. Maybe, if anyone complained about her now, it would mean another move. She could understand Bim's uneasiness about that.

The door to his room was closed. For a moment Monnie hesitated there. She felt, as she never had before, a need to talk with someone. And Bim seemed to have become a part of all the strange things that had happened.

But she did not linger. Instead she went on to the kitchen and, drinking her milk, told herself that whether he had a part in it or not, she was not going to join forces with Bim. She would face this alone, as she always had.

Friday was the bazaar and Mrs. Johnson was on the committee. She had to be there early, and she made both children promise to eat the sandwiches left wrapped in the fridge for lunch and then come on to the church. But that left their morning free.

Monnie could not make up her mind about the mailbox. She had not dreamed that odd dream last night—the one where she had been in the junk lot and had seen the star blazing on the front of the box. Did that mean there was nothing there for her? She wanted to go and make sure, but she was aware that Bim, even though he had gone back to his room with the excuse that he had to study for the test, had left his door open a crack. She was sure that if she left the house he would follow.

Still she could not stay home. The pull on her was so strong that at last, with a forbidding scowl at Bim's door, she went. There was no use dodging around trying to hide, she was sure he would guess exactly what she was doing. So Monnie went straight to the mailbox.

And—the flag *was* up!

But she hesitated a long time before she reached out to the lid. Queer things had happened to both her and Bim. Also she could not forget the face the doll had showed her last night—that old face.

Whose face? And why?

Monnie clasped her hands together so tightly the fingers ached.

Should she open the box? She wanted to, and she did not. It was so hard to make up her mind.

"What's there this time?"

Monnie's scowl grew blacker. Bim had followed her, but then she was sure that he would.

"Go ahead!" His voice sounded shrill. She would not look at him. "Maybe"—his arm shot past her shoulder as he reached out to tug at the lid—"it's for me. I need something lucky. . . ."

But the lid held tight. With a determined shove Monnie pushed him away. She was as sure that what lay inside was for her as if she could already see her name printed on the now-familiar purple envelope.

"It's mine," she said flatly and gave a tug to the lid, which opened easily as she touched it.

There was the letter—or at least the envelope with her name on it. And the same silver printing in the left corner, the stars in the right. Only this time there were five of them and the envelope itself felt heavier than the earlier ones she had found.

"Open it!" Bim urged. "Let's see what it is!"

Now that it lay in her hold Monnie was suddenly as eager as he to find out what had come so mysteriously. She picked open one end of the envelope, and there slid out, to lie on her other hand, a mirror.

The frame was silvery, with a pattern of queer markings, but the surface was as clear as the face

99

of the Voo-don't doll. The square of paper in which it was wrapped seemed to open all of itself to show her the words: "To see ourselves."

Bim read the sentence aloud. "What's that mean?" he demanded. "Sure you see yourself in a mirror, don't you? What's that going to do for you?"

Monnie raised the mirror a little and looked directly into it. She saw her reflection, yes, but that only lasted for a moment. A haze spread across the mirror—it was like fog. The mist did not stay on that flat surface but arose like smoke out of a fire.

With a cry Monnie dropped the mirror on the ground and edged swiftly back. The mist thickened. There was more and more of it. Now it began to change color, too. It was no longer gray-white. Part of it was faded blue, part of it was dark brown—just the shade of Monnie's own hair.

Now the mist. . . . No—there was no mist—there was Monnie—a second Monnie looking just as real as herself. The new Monnie was scowling at her and now made a nasty face.

"Who are you?" Monnie demanded.

The mirror girl laughed. "I'm Monnie Fitts," she declared. "Ask Bim!"

Monnie glared quickly in the direction the mirror girl had pointed. Bim was standing there, his eyes wide, his face so pale that he looked sick.

"I'm Monnie," the girl said again and advanced a step toward Bim. "It's true, isn't it? Say it, Bim—I'm Monnie!"

But Bim only covered his face with his hands and stumbled back.

"Make it go away!" his voice shrilled. "Make it go away!"

The mirror girl laughed again, jeeringly. "Why should I? I'm Monnie—Monnie Fitts. You know me—why don't you admit it, Bim?"

Bim ran, faster even than if Matt and all his gang had nearly caught him and were now at his heels. The mirror girl laughed for the third time.

"Yellow—plain yellow right through," she commented, giving voice to a thought Monnie herself had had once in a while. Bim was a better runner than a fighter.

But now Monnie herself tried to fight the fear that nearly made her go pounding after Bim. She was herself—Monnie Fitts! Therefore this other one was not Monnie—she was just a reflection that had somehow gotten out of the mirror.

"I'm real, you know." The girl came toward Monnie and held out her hand. "Give me a pinch if you don't believe that."

Not for anything in the world would Monnie have reached out to touch that—that *thing* that looked, talked, and seemed herself.

"You are *not* real!" Monnie's voice quivered,

she could not make it sound as if she were telling the truth.

The mirror girl made another face. "So? We'll see—oh, won't we just see!"

"Go away!" Monnie saw a wink of light in the tangle of dead grass. Though she hated to touch the thing she grabbed up the mirror. "Go away!"

"Sure. Just what I want to do." The mirror-Monnie turned and walked away, leaving her double by the mailbox with the mirror in her hand. A moment later she had disappeared around the wrecked car; Monnie was alone. She was shaking so hard now she nearly dropped the mirror. No—she must not break it. She had a strong feeling if anything happened to the mirror the second Monnie would be here always. Or was it already true and she would never be rid of that terrible other Monnie?

So far the gifts that the mailbox had brought had not been bad. Monnie drew a long breath and tried to remember that. The broom—that had done her no harm. And the Voo-don't doll—that had done some good. Stella had gotten the promotion at work—and Selma no longer twisted her hair and had been friendly. Only the dress for Mrs. Johnson had not come.

Though Bim's gifts had played tricks, they had not been bad ones. The bus door one had not lasted and the change in the exam had not really hurt anyone. The candle, perhaps, had prevented a fire from starting when that wire had been pulled loose.

But the mirror! Monnie continued to shiver. Suppose *that* Monnie went back to the apartment and said she lived there—acted as if she did. Bim would not tell. He had been too frightened, Monnie was sure. Then—where would Monnie go?

She could not just stay here. Putting the mirror back in its envelope, she stuck it in the back pocket of her jeans. Where could she go? The old house! Yes, nobody, even Bim, would look for her there—nobody knew about it.

Monnie ran. But as she went she wondered what the other Monnie was doing. Suppose she did something really bad? Monnie's memory supplied some pictures from the past of things she had done, or thought of doing. If the mirror-Monnie knew about those—why, she could do *anything* and then disappear and leave the real Monnie—her—to take the blame!

She rounded the tumbled-down old store and came to the little house. Her side hurt she had run so fast. And her thoughts hurt even worse as she imagined what might be happening back at the apartment with that Monnie there. She had to. stop her somehow—get her back into the mirror. But how could she possibly do that?

Monnie dropped down on the floor before the wide opening of the old fireplace. She could look up and see those seven stars carved along the wide stretch of the mantel above her head. And she found herself talking—as if there were someone here she could depend upon for help, someone she dared tell every part of this wild adventure to, tell it and be believed.

"I've got to get her back," she repeated at the end of the story she had poured out to the air and the fireplace. "I don't know what she might do. She isn't me—I'm the real Monnie."

Now she took out of hiding her three gifts from the mailbox.

"See? I'll give everything back—just let it be like it was before. Just fix it so she can't do. . . ." Monnie, for the first time in years, cried, covering her face with her hands. She could think clearly, and she did, of all of the awful things that other Monnie could do—things she had wanted to do to Bim, to Stella, to the girls at school, to—to everybody in the world, where she was always alone and unhappy.

"Just let me get her back," she said in a whisper. "Get her back before. . . !"

She hesitated and then made herself say it, "Before she does all those things I wanted to do. She—I don't believe she's afraid of doing anything!"

# 8

---

## See Yourself!

Monnie did not know what kind of an answer she had so faintly hoped to hear. As if there were anyone listening anyway! Slowly her thoughts began to sort themselves out and she did not shiver so much. It—maybe all that had happened was not real after all! Maybe this was just a dream, like those others she had had when she had been in the junk lot and seen the stars blaze on the front of the mailbox.

The mailbox!

Monnie set her teeth with grim determination. If there was not any mailbox, then maybe all the rest of the things would be gone, too—what both she and Bim had taken from that battered box.

Suppose she just smashed that old mailbox—smashed it flat—and then threw it away?

Monnie got to her feet eagerly. That was just what she was going to do.

Only . . .

When she tried to turn toward the door it was as if she had her feet caught in some stiff glue—or cement. Fear flared up again. She could not move!

"Please!" She cried it aloud. But there was no one she could see, no one at all! She twisted and turned her body, but her feet were fixed solidly to the floor.

Monnie felt sick. What was going to happen to her? Why was she stuck in this old house? She wanted to scream her loudest but now she felt as if she could not make any sound, even the lowest of whispers.

Because she was so sick and dizzy she folded up on the floor once more, her hands over her eyes. She was being kept here—maybe so that other Monnie could do all those awful things that had crossed Monnie's own mind. To see herself—that was what the paper with the mirror had said. She saw herself—or part of herself—and she was so afraid.

Fumbling, she opened her wallet and laid the Voo-don't doll, blank face up, on the hearthstone. Then she lifted the chain from her neck and put the broom beside the doll. Last of all, though she never wanted to see it again, she set the mirror in a line with the other things from the mailbox.

"Take them back," she croaked again, her voice a harsh whisper. "Please take them back and just let me alone!"

The silvery color of all three objects glittered as brightly as if the sun was shining full on them. And Monnie discovered that, in spite of what she wanted, which was never to see any of them again, she was staring down at them.

There was a change in the Voo-don't doll! Once more a face formed there. Monnie wanted to scream, but she could not make a sound. For the face was her own. Her own, yes, but also different. She looked older—as if she were as grown-up as Stella, and the face kept on changing. Now—now she looked as old as Miss Reeder—as old as . . . Lines deepened around the eyes, the mouth, the hair turned gray and then white. Now it was the face of an old woman—the old woman she had seen once before.

The doll's mouth moved, the lips shaped words: "Be ready."

Monnie's breath caught in a half-sob. "Ready for what?" she demanded wildly. "Tell me—tell me how I can get her back in the mirror!" She did not know why she believed that the old woman doll could tell her that, but she was sure that she could.

107

"See yourself," the lips told her.

Her hands shaking so that she had to take both of them to pick up the mirror, Monnie obeyed because she could not help it. She stared straight into the mirror and saw. . . .

Nothing!

The surface remained bright and clear and all she could see in it was the wall of the old house behind her, even a bit of the outside beyond the doorless opening. Only she was not there!

"I'm—I'm gone!" she whispered.

Now she looked again to the doll, half expecting that the woman's face would be gone too. But it was not.

"I can't see myself," she told the doll.

"See yourself," those wrinkled lips repeated.

Again Monnie tried. The wall, the door—both were clear. She looked over her shoulder to make sure of that—that she was just not looking at some kind of picture. Yes, they were exactly what she was seeing with her own eyes when she turned her head. But she was not there.

"I'm not there!"

"See yourself."

Monnie cried out and grabbed the doll, to stuff it back in her wallet. The broom went with it. She wanted to leave the mirror where it lay on the stone, but somehow she dared not. Take them all back—back to the mailbox! That was what she must do.

108

Her feet were free again, and she ran with the same speed as when she had gone to the house—this time back to the junk-strewn lot. There sat the mailbox just as she had propped it up. The flag was down, the lid closed. Monnie caught at the twisted handle and pulled with all her strength. But it would not open. She thought of leaving broom, doll, and mirror right in front of it, but she found that, no matter how much she willed her hands to pull them out and drop them there, she could not do it.

Now fear gave way to anger and Monnie pounded with her fist against the stubborn lid.

"Open up!" she cried as if her voice could make it yield.

At last she realized that it wasn't going to work. That old lid was as tightly shut as if it were glued to stay that way forever and ever. Slowly she picked up broom, mirror, doll and put all three in her wallet.

She would have to go home—back to the project. She would have to learn what that other Monnie had done, the Monnie that was part of herself.

But she did not hurry, and as she went she tried to think. What would happen if people saw two Monnies together? How could she explain? There was no way. . . .

She came to the apartment and started reluctanly down the hall.

"Hey!"

Monnie jumped and half turned. Bim stood there. He had been hidden in the doorway of the Stevens' apartment. His face still had that queer color and he was shaking a little.

"She—she went upstairs," he said.

There was no need for him to say who "she" was. Monnie looked up the staircase and shivered almost as much as Bim. What was that other doing? Monnie thought again of the things that had crossed her mind sometimes when she had felt mean enough to want to get back at Stella for teasing or had been angry about some rule of the Johnsons.

"I've got to go and see," she said, more to herself than to Bim.

"Is—is she going to stay?" Bim wanted to know.

"I don't know." Monnie was forced into the truth. She began to climb toward the upper hall, listening, she was not sure for what.

Of course she had the door key and the apartment was locked, but somehow she had a feeling that no key or lock would mean anything to that other Monnie. And the door *was* still locked as she tried the knob.

She heard a shuffling behind her. Bim had followed, though she had not expected him to. Now she saw that he had in his hands both his gifts from the mailbox.

"Maybe," he said uncertainly, "if we give them all back. . . ."

Monnie shook her head. "I tried," she told him briefly. Then she opened the door. Once more she paused to listen. There was not a sound to be heard. Somehow the quiet made it even worse. She wanted to slam the door once more, turn and run.

But her one hope was to go ahead, face what was waiting for her.

There was no one in the living room, the Johnsons' bedroom was just as neat as Mrs. Johnson had left it this morning. Monnie gave a small sigh of relief. One of the things she had once thought of when Mrs. Johnson had been talking so much about neatness was making a real mess in there. But her own room—Stella's room—what could be going on behind *that* door now?

Monnie forced herself to reach for the knob and her fear made her throw the door open widely. She gazed in upon disaster!

The whole room looked as if someone had deliberately set out to make as much of a mess as possible. Bottles and jars had been swept from the top of the dressing table, the beds had been ripped apart, clothes were strewn over the floor. And, sitting cross-legged on Stella's stripped bed, was the mirror-Monnie. She was eating chocolates, grabbed with both hands from a box Stella had brought home the night before, and she grinned at Monnie.

"Good job, isn't it?" she demanded. "Just what we thought of that time when snooty nose was so mean about her old perfume. We poured *that* down the sink now! And just look at her fancy-ancy dress!"

She pointed a sticky finger at the soiled and rumpled heap of clothing, while Monnie recognized with a kind of horror Stella's new dress which was crowning the pile, its skirt smudged with lipstick, mixed with eye shadow.

"No!" Monnie tried to deny what she saw.

The other one laughed. "Yes. Wait till you see what we did to the kitchen! 'Be sure and put away the glasses after you wash them, Monnie'!" She said that like Mrs. Johnson when she was tired of telling Monnie what ought to be done. " 'Do your homework on time, dear. Be sure and take your heavy sweater. My, this isn't a very good report, Monnie. Hadn't you better try a little harder? Monnie, the hem's out of that skirt—wear your other one. And. . . .' " The mirror-Monnie grabbed two chocolates and stuffed them in her mouth at once so the rest came out in a muffled series of words. " 'No, you can't stay up and see *Champions*. No, you can't wear those jeans, Monnie, they're a disgrace! Monnie, leave Bim alone! Monnie, have you been into Stella's things again? Monnie, that's enough—enough—enough. . . .' "

"Stop it!" Monnie cried out. The words echoed in her head. All those things she *had* heard and they *had* made her mad.

"Always picking on us," the mirror-Monnie declared and threw the now-empty chocolate box across the room. "They're always picking on us, aren't they? All right, we're going to show them—aren't we now?"

*"You* did this—" said Monnie. "I didn't!"

"You—me—all the same," returned the other Monnie. She picked up an uncapped lipstick from the tumbled bed and sprawled on her stomach facing the wall where she scribbled or began to scribble until Monnie, anger conquering her fear, rushed across the room and struck at that hand.

But her fist passed through the other's as if there was nothing there at all.

"You aren't real!" she cried.

"Oh, yes, I'm real," countered the other. "I'm Monnie, too. And I can prove it. Do you remember. . . ."

Monnie listened and remembered. All the bad things that had happened—the library book, the time she was left out of the party when everyone else in the neighborhood was invited, the time she had saved all her money to buy the Barbie doll and had had to pay for the vase she broke, the time that. . . . All the things that had hurt and made her mad—every one of them.

She wanted to shut her ears the way someone shuts their eyes not to see something bad. But she had to listen.

*"They* can do anything they want, can't they?" chanted the mirror-Monnie, who still smiled that hateful smile. "And you can't stop them! You've wanted to do this for a long time." She made a sweeping gesture with one arm at all the mess in the bedroom. "You've wanted to show them. All right—now you have. And we aren't through yet, are we? Are we?" she demanded for a second time when Monnie did not answer.

"You can't—I won't let you!" she broke out fiercely. Seeing all this—it was different from just thinking about it. Stella's new dress she had been so proud of—ruined. All those marks on the wall. And *what* had been done in the kitchen? And this was not *her* fault, it was not!

It was as if the mirror-Monnie could read her mind.

"Oh, yes, it is! It's just what you wanted to do— only you were too scared to try. But now we aren't scared any more—we'll show them. Mrs. Johnson's room, that's next."

The mirror-Monnie slid off the bed. "Remember what you thought about two weeks ago— that will be fun!"

Monnie remembered now only too clearly. "No!" she shouted.

"But you want to, you know you do," said the mirror-Monnie.

"I don't," Monnie denied. "No, I don't! Mrs. Johnson—she's—"

"She's picky and she orders you around and she's always asking you questions," prompted the mirror-Monnie. "You don't like her, you don't like Stella—you don't really like anybody at all, do you?"

"I hate you!" Monnie cried out. "I hate *you!*"

The mirror-Monnie nodded. And she never stopped smiling that nasty smile. "Of course you do. You hate me—you hate you—you hate everybody in the whole world. Come on now, let's show them—"

"No!" Monnie stood with her back to the door. "I'm not going to let you do that."

"But you thought about it, you wanted to do it."

"That was . . . I don't want to do it any more. I don't want *you*—go away!"

"I can't—I'm you, remember. I'm Monnie Fitts."

Monnie shook her head. "You aren't, you aren't! I won't let you be. I'll stop you—I'll. . . ." In sheer desperation she pulled out her wallet and fumbled until she had the mirror once more in her hand.

But this time she turned the reflecting surface

toward that other Monnie. The smile vanished from the other's face. She looked sly and angry both.

"You can't do that," she said sharply. "You can't put me back. I'm you and you're me. You can't get rid of me."

"I'm *not* you!" Monnie cried out, fear making her voice sound very high and shrill. "And you're not me, you're *not!*"

"You made me."

"Then I'm going to unmake you!" Monnie did not know exactly what she meant. But she held up the mirror on a level with the other's sulky face. "You get back in," she commanded, with only a very dim hope that she might be obeyed. "You get back in where you belong."

"I'm you." But the other Monnie did not sound so sure of herself any more as she said that.

"You're not! I won't let you be!" Monnie took one step and then another still holding the mirror at a level where the other must see her own face if she looked toward it at all. And now she was doing just that.

The mirror-Monnie shivered. "I'm you!" she repeated, but her voice sounded weak and trembly.

Monnie lost a little of her own fear. "You're not me, I'm not going to let you be."

"You'll find you can't change." The other

Monnie was beginning to look misty around the edges.

"I'm going to," Monnie returned fiercely. "I'm going to be me, Monnie Fitts, and you're not a part of me if I say 'no'."

The mirror-Monnie grew thinner, became mistier. Then it was as if a wind blew through the room and caught her up. The fog twirled toward the mirror, and though Monnie wanted to throw it from her, she held on tightly as the mist became a thin tongue, touched tip to the surface of the mirror, and was sucked away into the smooth surface. Monnie hurried to put it back into the envelope.

"She's gone—she's really gone!" Bim stood in the doorway of the room. "But just look what she did!"

Monnie looked around the horrible mess in the room. Her heart sank—there was no way, absolutely no way of ever erasing every trace of the mirror-Monnie's destruction. And how could she explain? No one would ever believe her, even if Bim backed up her story. She wanted to sit down and just bawl—but that would not do any good either.

"What are you going to do?" Bim wanted to know.

"Try and clean up—as much as I can," Monnie answered bleakly.

"Look here," he said awkwardly, "I can help—at least some."

Monnie looked at him in open surprise. "What for? You didn't do this."

"No, but you didn't either. And it isn't fair that they are going to blame you for it," he answered, to her further astonishment.

"I can't tell them," she pointed out. "And if you help pick up they may think you helped do it."

Suddenly he grinned at her. "Maybe if I used that mirror I'd get a Bim about as bad. Come on, let's see what we can do anyway."

They set to work and, for some reason, as Monnie started to untangle the general mess, she discovered that things were not as bad as they had first appeared. When she shook out Stella's dress and rehung it in the closet it was hardly creased at all and what she thought were stains were just smears of powder which brushed right off. With Bim's help she put the room to rights. Monnie gave a sigh of relief. Even that nasty lipstick writing came off when she rubbed a dampened tissue over it.

"Now I've got to go and see what she did in the kitchen," she said. "Look here." She opened her wallet and took out the money she had been saving for her Halloween mask. "Can you take this and get some more candy—a box just like this?" She shook the box the mirror-Monnie had

118

emptied. To look at it made her feel sick now—
as if she had indeed eaten all its contents.

"Yes," Bim agreed. "She won't be back, will
she?"

"No!" Monnie's reply was very firm. "She won't
be back—not if I can help it—ever!"

# 9

## Door to Nowhere

When she tackled the horrible mess left by the mirror-Monnie in the kitchen Monnie discovered that things could be put to rights here, too. She scrubbed and emptied trash, put what she could save back in the fridge. To her continued surprise, when Bim returned with the candy, he kept on helping. They were lucky, so lucky, Monnie knew, that Mrs. Johnson was at the bazaar and they had the house to themselves. At last, so tired her shoulders ached, Monnie sat down on one of the stools to give a last look around. The traces of the mirror-Monnie destruction were all gone.

Bim leaned against the table and looked at her squarely.

"Did you really want to do all that?" he asked.

Monnie nodded. "I guess so. Sometimes you just want to turn everything upside down, or smash something, or—"

Now it was Bim who nodded. "I know. Seems like you just *have* to—"

"But *I* never did, not really," Monnie reminded herself quickly. "I just thought about it." Then she shivered. It seemed that even thinking about things could bring on trouble.

"I couldn't look in that old mirror, not for a million dollars," Bim said now. "I. . . ." He shook his head, and then continued. "I guess I might let out a Bim who would do even worse. Though," he added thoughtfully, "I would like a Bim who could give Matt what for—"

"No!" Both of Monnie's hands flew to cover the wallet where it was in the pocket of her shirt. "You're not getting any chance to—"

"Don't want it!" Bim replied as swiftly. "Say— look at the time. We'd better get on over to the church or Mrs. Johnson will wonder where we are." He pointed to the wall clock.

It was near two. Monnie surveyed her dirty shirt and jeans. Better not go like this. She gave Bim a measuring look into the bargain.

"We'd better clean up. She wouldn't like us to come like this."

Bim surveyed his own dirty clothes which showed clearly the results of their recent labors.

"Okay. Say . . ." He hesitated at the door of the kitchen. "Have you heard anything?"

"Like what?"

"Like why Miss Valasco came to see Mrs. Johnson this week?" He ran his tongue across his lips and his eyes shifted quickly away from hers when Monnie looked up at him. She could guess what was in his mind.

"You think they're going to move you again?" Monnie asked.

Bim shrugged. "Don't know. But did you hear?" he repeated.

"No. Miss Reeder came early too."

"I kind of like it here," Bim said slowly. "The Johnsons aren't so bad. First time I ever had a room of my own. And Mr. Johnson—he's going to take me to Little League next season. If I'm here."

If I'm here! The words repeated themselves in Monnie's mind. She might have said them herself. She moved uneasily on the stool.

"If we're careful," she began slowly, "real careful—maybe they'll change their minds."

"Yeah. Maybe. . . ." But he did not sound too sure of it. Then he was gone. Monnie followed him more slowly, giving a last searching inspection to the kitchen. She had to be sure that everything was in place again.

Back in her room she also made sure that all the traces of the mirror-Monnie's destruction were gone and that the candy was where it had been. Queer how bad it had looked but how easily all the stains and spots had been wiped off.

Sweep clean. Out of nowhere the words slipped into her mind. Maybe it was having the broom that had helped wipe out the results of the mischief that other Monnie had left.

She shed her shirt and her jeans and put on a jumper and another shirt—the plaid one she wore to school. For the first time she sat down in front of the mirror—the *real* mirror—and worked with her stubborn hair, using comb and brush and bobby pins borrowed from Stella's supply.

The Monnie she looked at now *was* different! At least outside—and if that other Monnie *was* in her, then she had to be sure she did not get out again. She wrapped the mirror, being very careful not to look into it, in two tissues, and stowed it in her wallet. With hesitation she handled the broom and finally slipped the chain back around her neck, tucking the sliver of silver into hiding.

The doll she would not look at. It was too full of surprises—like the mirror. But she had been lucky, so lucky! Monnie drew a deep breath of pure relief. What if she had not had time to clean up? No, she was not even going to think about that!

Though she still had twinges of uneasiness for fear that Mrs. Johnson or Stella would notice something out of place when they came back from supper at the church, no one appeared to do so. The only unusual thing was that when Stella passed around her box of candy, Monnie refused a piece. She could not have forced it down. The way she felt at that moment, she never wanted to see a box of chocolates again!

She was so tired when she crawled into the upper bunk that she could not keep her eyes open. But still in the back of her mind she knew how lucky she had been. With that knowledge came uneasiness. Why had Miss Reeder come ahead of her regular time? And—worst of all—what if that other Monnie should come again? But she was not going to allow herself to think about that—she was not! All the next day she worried and tried not to think of what had happened. Mrs. Johnson appeared to be very absentminded, too. She never checked on Monnie's room-cleaning, and in the afternoon she took Bim off to get some new pajamas and shirts.

Monnie wondered about that. Were they going to move Bim? And if they did . . . now she felt a little sick and lost. Maybe it would mean she would have to go again, too.

But she was careful not to ask questions and was only too glad to go to bed even though it was Saturday night. This night she did not feel like playing the house game either, and it took her what seemed to be a long time to go to sleep.

It was dark and cold. Monnie shivered and tried

to pull the covers up around her shoulders more tightly. Only there were no covers. She was no longer in the bunk bed. It was dark—and there were all kinds of queer shadows reaching out. This was—the junk lot!

She stood by the wrecked car, but someone else squatted before the mailbox. In the very dim light she could not be sure, but she thought it was Bim. Bim! How could he dare to come again? The mirror—surely they had had enough trouble.

Monnie wanted to grab at the hand Bim was putting out to the lid of the mailbox. Her feet were bare, and she had only her worn robe on over her pajamas. This was a queer dream—it was too real. She *was* here, though she did not know how she had come. And Bim was, too.

He opened the box. Monnie's throat ached, she wanted so hard to scream at him, but she could not make a sound. Nor could she move. She had to stand there and watch Bim reach inside the box. He brought out a big envelope—so large a one that he had to wriggle it back and forth and do a lot of pulling to get it out at all.

It was purple, the six silver stars in the stamp corner glowed so brightly they were like little patches of light. Monnie could not see Bim's face, for he kept his head bent as he laid the envelope on the ground. For a long moment he made no effort to open it—perhaps because he was afraid,

Monnie thought, She was—after what had happened with the mirror.

Still she could not call out any warning or move toward Bim. He was only wearing his robe, also, and it was too small, so his hands stuck out of the sleeves, as well as part of his arms well above his wrist. Now he began to pry at the flap of the envelope.

With a last impatient jerk he had it open. Then he edged out its contents almost as if he expected something to bite him. Monnie squeezed her hands together and tried again to yell at him to let it alone—that there was going to be bad trouble. She was as sure of that as she was that she stood there shaking in the cold of the night.

Whatever was in the envelope did not come out easily. Bim had to pull and pry at it. Then he worked it loose at last and held it up. It was not another mirror as Monnie had half feared it might be. Instead Bim held a star—a five-pointed star —or rather the outline of one for it appeared to be made of wire.

The wire blazed with so bright a fire that Monnie heard Bim's gasp as he let it fall to the ground. Then. . . .

It was as if the wire of the star was alive! It lengthened and stretched out and out, until it was big enough for someone to stand in. And from where it lay on the ground there was a steady gleam of light rising from each of its points, as well as a lesser shine along the lengths of the wire uniting them.

Bim stood up. Now Monnie could see his face. To her amazement his eyes were closed. Nor did he open them as he took one step forward and then a second. It was as if he were walking in his sleep.

"Bim!" Somehow she had found her voice and shouted his name.

But he did not look in her direction at all. Instead he took a third step forward—into the space surrounded by the wire star. The lights at the points blazed even higher. Bim—she could see him for a moment, still standing there, his eyes closed—and then. . . .

Bim was gone!

Monnie stumbled forward, at last able to move. She reached the star. The light was beginning to fade. The star itself—it was growing smaller. But it had taken Bim! Before she thought Monnie jumped into the space at its center, which was hardly large enough now to hold her.

There was a blackness all about. And she was falling—no—not falling—but floating, or flying . . . she was not sure which. The feeling that there was nothing solid to hold on to made her sick at her stomach and more frightened than she had been even when the mirror-Monnie had come.

On she whirled through the dark. She threw out her arms, grasping with her hands, trying to find something to hold on to. But there was nothing at all except the dark and the air.

Bim's eyes opened slowly. He had been having a very strange dream. In it he had gotten out of bed, put on his robe, and walked right out of the apartment. Then there had been the mailbox, and somehow there was a star—a very big and shining star—and. . . .

He blinked as he looked up. But what was overhead was not the familiar ceiling of his small bedroom. Instead there was a shadow-hung ceiling with big beams across it. It was very dark except for a flickering of light coming from somewhere to his left. He moved his hands slowly. He was lying on something like a bed, at least it had covers but they were not the soft blankets he expected; they felt stiff and hard.

This must be part of the dream—but it was so queerly real.

Now Bim slowly turned his head toward the light. What he saw first was the fire—a real fire burning in so large a fireplace that it seemed to stretch nearly across one wall of the room. The fire was a small one in the very center of the big black cave that held it.

Above the fire was the overhang of a wide stone mantel and along that. . . .

Stars—seven of them. They were not silver

bright like the stars that had shone on the envelope—what envelope? Bim frowningly tried to remember. All that seemed faint and far away. A mailbox—yes, there had been a mailbox and that had had stars on it too.

The seven stars here glowed purplish. And the fire burning was real—he could feel the heat of it. Bim watched it for a minute or two and then looked down where he lay. This was certainly *not* the bed in which he had gone to sleep. It was even narrower and closer to the floor, so that the highest of these flames were on a level with his eyes.

Now, thoroughly uneasy and beginning to be frightened—because everything was so *real*—he sat up. There were no other lights in the room but the fire, so it was hard to see all of it. His low bed stood along the wall directly across from the fireplace. There were a table and some wooden stools and what seemed in this very uncertain light to be a big cupboard against the far wall.

From the ceiling overhead hung strings and bunches of what looked like dried weeds tied together. But there were onions, too, and some withered-looking peppers. Save for Bim himself there was no one else there.

Slowly he stood up, still straining to see into the far corners of the room. Nothing moved there. And because he was alone—though he was not

quite sure who or what he could expect to see—
Bim felt more at ease. Only, every time his eyes
flickered over those purple stars on the mantel
stone, he knew a stir of real fear. They meant trouble, of that Bim was sure.

He took a step and then another until he was
closer to the fire. For the first time he noticed
that he was not wearing pajamas, or even jeans
and a tee shirt. Instead he had on a pair of
breeches made of a material as stiff nearly as the
blankets on the bed. The bottoms of these were
tucked into thick stockings. Above the waist he
had on a shirt of checked stuff, brown and white,
a little too big so that the cuffs slid forward across
the back of his hands. It was gathered in around
his waist by a big leather belt.

Bim shook his head, closed his eyes, counted
to ten, and then opened them again. It was all the
same. But this was a dream—it had to be!

He reached out his right thumb and forefinger
and pinched hard at his left arm beneath the folds
of that strange shirt. He pinched so hard that he
gave a surprised sound though hardly more than
a squeak. That had *hurt!*

But how could this be real? And if it was,
where was he and how had he come here? Bim
stared at the fire without seeing it now. Instead
he was trying to think back. There was a mailbox
—that was important. What had happened?

Slowly it came to him—Monnie's box—and his. He remembered the Sa-boom wand, the silver candle. . . . Now he turned and hurried over to the bed. When he had gone to sleep in the real world those had been under his pillow. But there was no pillow on this bed, just a torn piece of blanket folded up. Bim pushed both hands under it and felt cool metal. He pulled them out—the two things from the mailbox were in his hands. Two? Something else slipped to the floor.

Bim stooped and picked up a star—a five-pointed star made of wire. The points were thicker than the rest and felt rough to his fingertips. The star was certainly strange enough to be something else from Seven Spells. Only he did not remember getting it.

Now he touched it very gingerly. Monnie's first two "gifts" had done no harm—but that mirror —and it had been her *third* find. He wanted nothing to happen to him as it had to her! Yet it was plain that the star did belong with the other two things. It was made of the same silver and seemed to shine in this dark room as if it held a light of its own.

This dark room. . . . Where *was* he? Bim edged slowly back to the fire. Not only its warmth, but the light it gave seemed somehow to make him feel better. But he would not look up at the stars on the mantel. He wet his lips with tongue tip and then tried out his voice. "Hello?"

He did not know what or who he expected would answer him. But there was no answer except the crackle of the fire. Then Bim noticed it was dying down. He looked around a little frantically. To be left alone in the dark—no! That must not happen. There was a pile of wood lengths—covered with bark and looking as if they had been part of a tree cut down not too long ago—at one side of the big hearth. Bim hurried to pull out a couple of them and shove them into the flames. For a moment he thought that he had put the fire out with his clumsiness. Then a twig standing up from the top length caught and began to burn and he gave a sigh of relief.

He watched anxiously until he was sure that the fire would continue to burn. Using all the courage he could summon, he turned away from the hearth and made a slow circle of the room, stopping now and again to look over his shoulder. For the feeling was growing stronger all the time that he was not alone, even though he could see no one at all.

There were two windows in the walls, but he could not see through them for they were covered with square wooden shutters, with a bar set across them to keep them so. A similar bar held the door shut from the inside. He found a couple of chests, mainly by bumping into them, and when, greatly daring, he opened the door of the cupboard, all he saw were crocks and jars, all tightly lidded, and some thick brown dishes.

His exploring done, he arrived back at the fireplace again. Now he sat down cross-legged, glad of the heat, for the farther portions of the room were cold. He had found at the side of the bed a pair of shoes which, when he tried them, fitted over his stockings. Queer shoes they were, with very thick soles and made so you could not tell the right from the left.

If this was not a dream, and more and more he was certain it was not, then Bim could not puzzle out what had happened to him. Now he laid out on the hearthstone, in the light of the fire, the things from the mailbox. The Sa-boom and the candle seemed like old friends. He put the star a little aside from them for he did not trust it in the least. Then, because he was *sure* that he was not alone, he turned his head.

Keeping one hand on the candle and Sa—boom he spoke aloud for the second time. "Please— where am I?"

He had lived in many different places, had started a new life many times in the past. But always there had been a likeness between those new starts. He had gone with Miss Valasco, there had been another apartment or house not too unlike the one from which he had come. But this—this was so different.

"Where am I?" he repeated, his fingers curling about Sa-boom and the candle, his heart thumping until it seemed to shake his whole body with every beat.

# 10

## Where Is Home?

There was a sudden up-spring of flame in the fireplace. Bim turned his head to look.

"So you've come back, Hosah?"

Bim whirled about the other way. She sat there on one of the stools which was so short-legged that she appeared to crouch. And the light from the flames made her very clear to see, though the long, bunchy dress she wore hid all but her head and neck.

She was really old, older than Mrs. Pritchett back at the project. Most of her head was hidden by a purple cap, but a few strands of white hair showed on her forehead and hung below the edge of the hood onto her neck. Her eyes . . . he could hardly see them because they were set so far back under bushy eyebrows. And her nose, which was big, curved out like the beak of a parrot he had once seen, making her mouth look smaller and tighter under the spread of it.

Her hands were busy knitting. Though her fingers moved fast and the click-click of her needles came steadily, she never looked down at her work, rather eyed Bim narrowly.

He scrambled up and back one step away, and then two. She was so unlike anyone from his own world that he was afraid, though she had made no threat, only sat there knitting. But where had she come from? The door, the windows were still tightly shut and barred. And his earlier explorations of the room had found no other opening.

"Welcome home." Now her small mouth opened farther and he could see the points of two yellowish teeth against the pale lips.

"I'm not. . . ." Bim began and then hesitated. Wherever he *was* it was certainly *not* home. But where was home? The Johnsons'? Yes, for now.

"Not quite yourself, Hosah?" The old woman was nodding and the folds of her big purple cap bobbed back and forth, throwing queer-shaped shadows against the wall. "Been a long trip maybe?"

Bim gathered what courage he had left. "I'm Bim Ross." He tried to announce it firmly, but his voice quavered in spite of his efforts. "And I want to go home."

The old woman shook her head. She pointed to him with one of her needles.

"Ha, Hosah, you can remember better than that, can't you now? Sit you down and think, lad, think!"

As if her will had called it out of the shadows, there was suddenly another stool there, and Bim sat down on it. He squeezed his hands close together between his knees. His heart was still beating fast and he gasped as if it were hard to breathe. This was worse than being caught by Matt and his gang.

"Drat!" Now the woman was looking at her knitting, picking at it with the point of the needle she had used to guide him to the stool. "A dropped stitch. Now that can't be allowed—a dropped stitch, a life-line gone all crooked."

For the first time Bim looked more closely at the knitting. It was a collection of many colors of yarn. Perhaps it was the dim light of the fire that made them look so faded. And whatever the thing was that she worked on it was very big, or long. It fell over the edge of her knees to lie in a coil on the floor, the colors running in and out of it in no pattern at all.

"Oh, but there is a pattern, Hosah." She had pushed the free needle into the end of the knitting she held. "Here's happiness, and here's sorrow, and good, and evil, and rain and shine, and growth and harvest, and beginnings and endings

139

—just as it should be. Black and white, red and blue, green and yellow. . . A bit of sky here, a dollop of stream there, a finger-scoop of earth, a leaf of plant, a flake of snow, a drip of ice, or rain, a patch of sun." . . . She singsonged all the words as if she were indeed singing them aloud.

And as she called out each—sky, stream, earth, leaf and all the rest—it seemed to Bim that one strand of her knitting: blue, silver-white, brown, or green, glowed brighter for an instant. But he held onto his own need to know.

"Where is this place?" he asked and raised his eyes, refusing longer to watch the flying needles in her hands.

"In its own time, Hosah, in its own time. Time can be place. Have you forgotten everything, lad? My, what a dullard you have chosen to become!"

She shook her head and her lips formed a visible tut-tut, though she did not utter it aloud.

Bim was stung by fear into sharp denial. "I'm Bim Ross not—not Hosah—whoever he is. And I want to go home."

"And where is home?" she asked then.

"Well, to the Johnsons'. At least that's where I'm living now."

"Now—then—time does not count. Not here. You have the wand, the candle, the star. Keys open—"

"I don't want them!" Quickly Bim laid the

three out on the hearth, where they began to shine quite dazzlingly.

"Ah, but you have no choice, Hosah. The spells are yours, for have you not made them yours by use?"

Bim shivered, warm as the fire which reached him was.

"Take them back!" he cried. "I'm Bim Ross, I don't want to be anyone else. I don't want to be here—let me go home!"

Now she laughed. "Impatient as always, Hosah. And as unheeding. If you meddle with magic, then you may be wedded to it. As for going back —that we shall see. But where is she who must complete the spell? I wonder now."

Once more she disengaged one of the needles from her knitting, sliding all her stitches onto the other one she held. With it she pointed, not to Bim again, but rather at the star of silver wire.

It trembled, arose from where it lay on the hearth, and, obeying the beckoning of the needle, flipped over to lie on the floor between their stools. Now the needle moved quickly in the air, pointing in turn to each of the points where the rays of the star met.

Light gleamed higher from those places and the star stretched larger and larger. Bim gave a little cry and edged his stool back. Then the woman spoke. "She is lost. This spell is yours. . . . Call her."

Call who? Bim was confused. Then he knew. Only Monnie could be the one who mattered. Where was she lost? And how—

"Call, lad—do you wish her to be always lost?" The woman's voice came sharper.

"Monnie . . ." Bim's voice sounded hardly louder than a whisper, a croaking whisper. "Monnie!" He tried to make it louder this time.

"Better than that, boy. You croak like a frog in the pond. Or is it that you do *want* to lose her?" The woman stabbed the air with her free needle.

If Monnie could be here! He did not want to lose her! She was real, a part of what he must find again. Bim drew a deep breath and now he shouted. "Monnie!"

The word rang around the room, seemed to echo, so that he heard the name not once but many times, bouncing back to him from the dark walls. The fire leaped higher and brighter.

Then in the center of the star there was a foggy ball. Suddenly Bim remembered the Monnie from the mirror. She had come the same way— and he did not want *her!* He watched, afraid again, as the fog streamed higher. Then it was gone.

There was someone there. She was crouched down in a kind of ball, her arms around her bent knees, her face pressed against them so he could see nothing but a tangle of hair hanging over her shoulders. But Monnie did not have long hair— at least not that long.

"Monnie?" Now he made a question of her name.

She was shivering hard enough for him to see it. And she was not wearing Monnie's jeans and shirt, or even her best jumper and blouse. Instead, what she had on looked bunchy and queer—and it was of a dull brown color, nearly the same shade as her hair so you could not see where her hair ended and the dress began. If she heard him call her name she made no move to answer.

"Monnie?" He spoke louder.

"I won't look, I won't!" Her voice was muffled for she did not raise her head. "It's all queer and black and I won't look!"

"Monnie—it's me, Bim." He grew impatient. "You better believe it. . . ."

Very slowly her head came up and he could see Monnie's face, but her eyes were squeezed very tightly shut.

"I won't look!" she repeated. "I can't look."

"Yes, you can!"

As Bim spoke there was a small ring of sound. The star shape in which Monnie crouched arose in the air, hovered just over the girl's head. Once more it grew smaller, became the wire piece Bim had laid on the hearth. Then it sped back there, to settle beside the wand and the candle.

"Welcome, Hannah." The old woman inserted her needle once more into her knitting and began the work she did not watch at an even faster rate, as if she must make up for lost time.

Monnie's eyes came open. She stared at the fire. Then, not looking in Bim's direction at all, she turned her head to face the old woman.

"I—I know you . . ." she said slowly. "You are the Voo-don't doll!"

"Am I now?" The woman laughed. "No, I am hardly a doll, Hannah."

"I am not Hannah." Monnie's jaw thrust forward stubbornly in a way Bim knew very well. "I'm Monnie Fitts!"

"So you said—or proclaimed yourself in writing." The woman nodded. "Well, Monnie, here you are Hannah. And why have you chosen to pay us a visit? This was not your spell—"

"Bim. . . ." Now Monnie did look around. "You *are* here, Bim!" She sounded angry as if she were awfully mad at him. "What did you do to us? Where is this place?"

Before he could answer, the old woman laughed, and to Bim her laugh sounded unpleasant.

"But *you* know where you are, Hannah. Look about you, girl, use your two eyes!"

Monnie remained where she was, hunched up just as she had appeared in the star. But now she turned her head slowly, even moving partway around without getting up so she could see the room. She was frowning, not as if she were still mad at Bim, but rather, he thought, as if she were trying to remember something.

And Monnie was. She had been in the cold dark, which had frightened her worse than she had ever been frightened in her whole life—mainly because she felt that perhaps she was going to be left there forever and ever. Then—then she had come here and heard Bim calling her name.

The old woman had been the doll (or at least a face for the doll, Monnie was sure of that). And this place. . . . She lifted her head a little higher and saw them—the stars set in the mantel above the warmth of the fire.

"This is the old house," she said, sure she was right. "But—but it's different—it's a regular house again. You—" Now she looked directly at the woman. "You live here, don't you?"

"I live here—you might say that. Or at least I live in the house that is now—"

"Is now?" Monnie repeated questioningly.

It was changed, of course. The door was there, and there was furniture about, though it was not at all as she had pictured it being.

"Monnie." Bim broke into her wonder. "She's crazy! She says you're Hannah and I'm somebody called Hosah and. . . . Monnie, we've got to get back home."

Monnie looked back directly at the woman. "Why do you call me Hannah?" she asked.

"Why do you call yourself Monnie?"

"Because that's my name!"

"Are you sure?" the woman asked surprisingly.

"Of course, I'm sure!" Monnie returned. "And he's Bim—Bim Ross. And where are we anyway?"

"Where do you want most to be?"

Monnie was startled by that question. Where did she want to be?

"Home!" She answered that quickly.

"Yes, home!" Bim echoed her eagerly. "Just let us go home!"

"And where is home?"

Monnie opened her mouth. But what she had been about to say—the project—the Johnsons' apartment. . . . No, that was not home. Home was the place she clung to at night when she pictured her private dream—the dream she was sure would never come true for her.

"You see"—the old woman was reading her thoughts—"you don't even know where this home you want is—now do you?"

"She does." Bim's voice sounded strained. "Tell her, Monnie! We're with the Johnsons—we want to go back—"

"We're at the Johnsons'," agreed Monnie slowly. "But that isn't home—not really, Bim."

His face was flushed and both of his hands were balled into fists as if he longed to pound her. But now he blinked and his eyes no longer met hers.

146

"I don't care—I want to go back . . ." he said in a low voice.

"You brought the keys. . . ." The woman's needle now pointed to the three things on the hearth and Monnie felt a stir in the waist of the queer, long-skirted, bunchy dress she now wore. Before she could reach and hold what lay beneath it, they pushed out of hiding just below her chin and flew through the air to join Bim's things, the broom, the Voo-don't doll, the mirror, now free of the covering she had so carefully wrapped about it.

"The rest is up to you," the woman said.

Monnie looked from her to the six silver things on the hearthstone and then back to the woman. But she was no longer looking at either child. From a bag which hung on long strings from her belt she had pulled another piece of thin wool, this one a dull red, and was busy knotting it fast to the piece she had been using which was very close to the end of its length.

"What rest?" Monnie wanted to pull the knitting out of the woman's hands, make her explain.

"You will see," was all the answer she got. And her anger grew. But the woman did not even look up at her now and somehow Monnie did not quite dare to pull at the other's skirt or do as she wished and grab the knitting.

Do as she wished! Monnie's gaze snapped back to the mirror on the hearth. What if her thoughts did come true—as the mirror-Monnie had proven that they could?

The broom, the doll, the mirror—the old woman had called them keys, if Monnie had understood her right. Keys to what? They were not in the least like the key to the Johnsons' apartment.

"How do we get back?" Bim asked that, not of the woman, but of Monnie.

"I don't know." She told him the truth. "At least not yet."

"Think. . . ." The old woman had knotted her yarn firmly together and her needles were flashing again. They moved so fast it seemed that no fingers could ever hold them, as if they were part of a machine that worked by itself. And as they moved they gave off sparks—purplish sparks. The flying sparks became brighter and brighter, and there were more and more of them. Until all Monnie and Bim could see was a rain of sparks shooting out into the air.

Then—they all vanished. And there was no one there—just a stool pulled up comfortably close to the fire. The old woman and her coils of knitting were gone.

Bim was on his feet. "She can't do this!" He swung around and caught up the wand from the hearth. What he might do with it he had no idea but he pointed it at that empty stool and shouted, "Sa-boom!"

If there had ever been any power in the wand,

if it had locked the bus door and changed the test papers, it did not work now. He shook it and then tossed it back to lie beside the other things.

"We've got to find our own way back—I think. . . ." Monnie said slowly.

"The star—it got us here, didn't it!" Bim clutched at the piece of shaped wire. He dropped it on the floor and waited. But there was no change in it this time. It did not shine more brightly at the corners, nor did it grow.

"It isn't going to be that easy." Monnie spoke her thoughts aloud. She regarded her own three gifts carefully but did not move to touch them. Broom, doll, mirror—they must have a meaning just as Bim's things did. If she could only catch that meaning—just a hint which might lead her to it.

"We got to get back!" Bim's hands were shaking. "Something is going to happen—something is—"

He was right. Monnie could feel it now, too. She turned quickly to look at one shadowed corner of the room and then the next. There was a waiting feeling, a bad waiting feeling. She had known this before—it was like when Miss Reeder came to move her to a new foster home. Changes —bad things—happened when there were a lot of changes.

Now it was as if something pointed her straight

at the barred door—whatever was on its way was going to come from that direction. And soon.

She looked at the vacant stool where the old woman had been. No use calling for her, Monnie was sure of that. Whatever came now the two of them had to face and alone. The two of them. . . . Now she looked straight at Bim, Bim who ran from Matt and his gang, who she had always believed had no more courage than a crybaby.

To her surprise he was facing the door also, and there was a queer, set expression on his face which made him somehow look stronger than she had ever seen him before.

"We got to—" To do what, she could not say.

Before she found the right words, Bim had turned back to the hearth and was scooping up star, candle and wand. He pointed with his chin to her own things.

"We'll need 'em!" he said with a force that carried to her the belief that somehow he was speaking the truth.

# 11

---

## Broom and Wand, Mirror and Star

Very reluctantly Monnie moved to pick up her own three gifts—if they were gifts at all. They felt warm in her hands, but that was because, she thought, they had lain so close to the fire.

Bim still faced the door. He held the wand in one hand, the star and the candle in the other. The tip of the wand was now pointing toward the bar on the door.

It—it was moving!

Monnie pushed closer to Bim. As he had done, she gathered doll and broom into her left hand and with her right held up the mirror, its smooth surface turned well away to face the doorway. The bar arose as if a hand they could not see was moving it. Then it tilted, to thud one end to the floor.

Something—something—stood outside, was making this happen! Monnie found herself breathing in small, hurried gasps. This was worse than any dream she had ever had to torment her. Her arm was pressed against Bim's, she stood so close to him, and she could feel the shivers running through him, too.

Though the door had unbarred itself—or something unseen had unbarred it—it had not yet opened. And out of somewhere words sped into Bim's head. He repeated them aloud as if he were not really a part of what was going to happen, but just a tool—like a hammer or a saw—which someone was about to use. Which was a queer thought, but one he did not have time to understand now.

> "Oak for the door,
>    More for the floor.
> Ash and Rowan near—
>    By the power within this wand
> No harm will enter here."

His voice rang out, and as when he shouted for Monnie, it echoed back to him queerly from the corners of the room. He did not know where he had learned those words, but at that moment Bim was very sure that he *had* learned them once. Just as he had also stood like this—in this very same room—and faced. . . .

Monnie's voice followed before the echoes of his had quite died away.

> "Silver of moon,
>     Silver of mirror
> Be without as within—
>     One man's joy,
> Another's sin."

The door crashed open with a mighty force which sent it slamming back against the wall. At the same time light flashed from the wand and the mirror, to show what stood there.

"No!" Monnie cried out first in denial.

For there was the mirror-Monnie—or at least a figure that looked like her—a Monnie with tangled hair, a scowling face, jeans ripped on one knee, and a dirty shirt.

And beside the mirror-Monnie whom she had thought safely gone, was a Bim—a Bim with the familiar smudge under his nose, the shifting eyes, the slinking sort of walk.

But she could feel Bim still beside her! And she was Monnie—she really was!

The two in the doorway came in, Monnie with a challenging tramp, Bim, a little behind, as if he feared something was about to leap at him. But they were not alone.

Shadows streamed behind them. And, as she looked at each of those in turn, a face arose out of Monnie's memory, a face she did not want to see again. They meant hurt or anger. Seeing one or two of those shadows made her redden with shame. These were not just thoughts that the mirror-Monnie carried out, these made her think of things she had actually done.

Not all the shadows were hers, but those that must be Bim's were so thin she could not make out their faces. Perhaps it was meant that they see only their own.

The other Monnie held out her hands.

"Come on," she commanded. "Come back where you belong. You wanted to go back. We'll show you the way."

The shadows behind her began to flow together, growing darker, stronger. Then they melted into the waiting Monnie, so that she grew taller, and, as Monnie herself knew, stronger. Soon she would actually touch Monnie—and when she did—

"No!" Monnie denied the power of that other.

"Yes!" The second Monnie nodded her head. "You wanted to go back—it's easy—just take my hand. . . ."

Then Monnie knew. If she did take that hand held out to her, she would go back, yes—and all the darkness in the other would be a part of her, just as the mirror-Monnie would always be inside

154

her—waiting, along with all those others, waiting
for a chance to be the real Monnie.

Bim held the wand so tightly his fingers ached.
He looked at that other Bim and the shadows behind him. And he remembered—the times he had
lied because he was afraid, the times he had run
because he was afraid, the time—the time he had
taken money from little Katie's bank because he
was afraid to admit he had lost the quarter given
to him to get stamps, the time. . . .

And the shadow Bims who had done all those
things moved closer and closer to the Bim who
had come through the door—they stepped into
him in a strange way, became a part of him. Then
that other Bim grinned at him.

"You want to go back? That's easy—just come
along—"

Bim pointed his wand at that other Bim. "You
aren't me!" His protest was shrill.

"Of course, I am. You know it."

It was true—that was Bim standing there—the
real Bim. Then what was he? Bim felt as if a great
cold wind had wrapped around him. What *was*
he?

"You're not real," that other Bim said, his grin
growing plainer. "You're just Hosah, remember?
I'm the real one—"

"You're not!" Bim's protest came again, but
less strongly.

"Throw that away." The other Bim pointed to

the wand. "Dump those other things—you'll never get back if you hold on to them—"

It was Monnie who answered. "Don't, Bim."

"They are real." His voice was hardly above a whisper now. "You know they are—"

"But so are we." Monnie raised her hand holding the mirror a little higher. "We are ourselves, Bim."

"She's crazy," said the other Bim. "You saw —we are real—you aren't. If you want to go back then come along."

"Not with you!" Monnie answered, and then added to Bim beside her, "Don't let them take you, Bim. Do you want to be a part of *them?*"

He looked at the Bim who had come through the door. And what he saw (all the other Bim shadows that had faded into him and now, one after another, seemed to look out of that too familiar face) frightened him.

The other Bim took another step forward. "You can't get away, you know," he said and his voice sounded like Matt's when he got Bim cornered in some doorway. "We can take you easy."

Bim's mouth felt dry. He could not answer now. Nor did he even dare to glance at Monnie. That other Bim was right, he was stronger, bigger, tougher, even though he might not look it. Bim could feel his toughness. He had. . . .

The wand in Bim's hand trembled and the point quivered toward the floor. He could no longer feel Monnie's arm against him. It was as if she had stepped back and away from him, withdrawing even the small bit of comfort caused by her being caught in the same danger with him. He was alone—except for that Bim who was reaching for him.

The shadows swept across that Bim's face one after another and Bim watched them, feeling sick. They were a part of him, he could never outrun them, just as he could not outrun the Bim who was going to take him.

Run? He had always been running. From the very start he had always run, and hid, and lied, and been all those Bims. Always afraid—that was Bim Ross. But he did not want to be that—not any more.

He forced his hand to quit shaking. The grin vanished from the other Bim's face. Now he looked bad—strong and bad like Matt. He *was* Matt!

"No!" Now it was Bim's turn to deny what he saw—this other Bim who had turned into Matt, raising his fists ready to move in on him. Without thinking, Bim made his choice, a wild one, but one he could not deny. He dropped the wand, the candle and the star. Awkwardly he raised his own hands now balled into fists.

"I'm not running—I'm not going. . . ." He struck out blindly at the Matt-Bim moving purposefully toward him.

Monnie had felt Bim's withdrawal. She saw that the other Monnie had taken advantage of her desire to keep Bim fighting and had come almost within touching distance of her. Why did she want to make Bim fight back? What was it to her that he must try to save himself? He was. . . .

She shook her head. That was a thought from the other Monnie, thrown to catch her as a rope could catch a horse. It was a mirror-Monnie thought.

"You are me," the other Monnie said. "You can't get rid of me, you know." She nodded as if that were a truth no one could deny.

"I have a choice," Monnie said.

Now she gripped the mirror more fiercely, slanted it a little, though the fear of what she was going to do was so strong she thought she never could carry through the act. Deliberately she turned the mirror around. It no longer faced the other Monnie with its shining surface, but reflected her own face. She waited for the spell to act— for a second Monnie, or a third, to come out of that gleaming disk. But all she saw therein was her own pale face and flying tangle of hair.

"I see myself," she said firmly. And she continued to look into the mirror, waiting for what she did not know. Perhaps another Monnie to walk out of the mirror, or perhaps the one she faced to seize upon her.

But nothing happened. Only her face was reflected there. It seemed that time stretched. Her hand dropped, taking the mirror away. There was no one there—no other Monnie—no other Bim.

On his knees a little away from her was the Bim she had found here. He had his hands over his face and she thought for a moment he was crying, only when he moved, raising his head and looking around, she saw that there were no tear marks on his cheeks. But he looked—different.

"I did it," he said slowly. "I quit running. I—I fought back! I wasn't *that* Bim any more."

"We're still here . . ." Monnie thought of the threat those others had made, that they would be left here.

But. . . .

The room had changed. There was no fire on the hearth warm behind them; the furniture was gone, the windows were gaping holes and so was the door. She looked down at her hands. The broom, the doll, the mirror—they had all vanished.

"We're back. But. . . ."

Monnie knew Bim's new fear before he spoke it. "They didn't bring us," she said quickly.

He drew a deep breath which was almost a sob. "Sure?"

"I'm sure." Monnie was firm about that.

"What—what did it all mean, then? Why?" Monnie shook her head. "I don't know."

Bim looked down at himself—he wasn't wearing the heavy clothing he had had on when he awoke in the low bed that was no longer there. Instead he wore his pajamas and robe, and there were slippers on his feet. He saw them, not by the light of the vanished fire, but by a grayish glimmer, which came in through the window holes and the place where the door had once hung. It was cold, very cold.

And Monnie—she had on pajamas and robe too, as if she had just gotten out of bed. Her hair was shorter, not as it was when she had appeared at his call in the middle of the star.

The star! He looked quickly at the floor. Nothing lay there.

"They're gone!" A flash of fear followed that realization. He wanted to hold the gifts again, even if it meant trouble.

"I know," Monnie answered him. "Mine, too. And . . ." She had half turned and was looking at the fireplace. "The stars. . . ."

"What stars?"

She pointed up to the heavy overhang of the mantel. "The ones up there—there were seven of them."

"She kept calling me Hosah—that old woman. . . ." Bim tried to remember back beyond the coming of that other Bim and his troubling shadows.

"I wonder what she was knitting . . ." Monnie said slowly. "All those colors. . . ."

160

"She said queer things," Bim answered. "Come on—I want to go home—it's cold!"

Monnie went to the door very slowly, as if she did not quite care about leaving. She looked back once more at the cold and empty hearth.

"Broom and wand," she said, "mirror and star."

Bim stared at her. "What's all that mean?"

"I don't know—it was just in my head all of a sudden," she told him. "I wish I knew more about her—that old lady."

"I don't!" Bim returned sharply. "Let's go. Say —it's nearly morning. We must have been here all night." He was already out of the door. "We'd better beat it quick before anyone sees us!"

Monnie hurried after. They sped across the street and were in the junk-strewn lot. It must be very early, Monnie decided. The streetlights were still on and there were a lot of shadows around.

But no shadow hid the mailbox. There it sat upright just as she had wedged it. And in spite of the dim light she could read their two names. And . . .

The flag was up!

"Bim!" Her call was so urgent that he stopped and looked back at her. Monnie pointed to the box.

"There's something there!"

He started to back away as if the mailbox itself was a danger he had no desire to face. Then he stopped, and that firm look Monnie had seen him wear when he faced the opening door of the house returned to his face.

"I don't want to," he said as if to himself, "but. . . ."

Step by slow step as if he were being pulled against his will, Bim drew nearer to the box. Monnie was already on her knees beside it. One part of her wanted to pull down the lid, another warned against what might happen then. But there had been seven stars—though now. . . . No matter how closely she looked she could not see a single one still painted on the front, only their two names—Monnie Fitts—Bim Ross.

Seven stars—and they had only six things. If there was a seventh gift which one of them was it for—Monnie or Bim? She was certain that there was something inside.

"Well, what're you waiting for?" Bim demanded. "Open it!"

She pulled against the lid but it was tight shut. "It won't open!"

"Let me." Bim crowded down beside her. But as his hand joined hers on the lid, it fell open. And there was no letter—but a package inside. Not wrapped in the purple paper this time either, it was more like an untidy bundle of knitting about the size of their two fists put together.

Monnie reached in. As she pulled it into the very dim light of early morning the knitting fell

162

away; the strands of colored wool, if they were wool at all, seeming to wither like old leaves into an ashy nothingness.

What was left was a round ball, but as Monnie held it up higher so they could see it better, it split into two parts. Each formed a dome of clear glass, holding tight within it a house. It was different, Monnie could see, from the house behind the old store, but it was also built of stone. And there was something familiar about it. Her breath caught. Why shouldn't she know this house—these houses, for there was one exactly like it in the other dome.

This was the house she had planned in her head all those nights in bed when sleep wouldn't come and she had wanted, so fiercely, a place of her own. There was the sharp-peaked roof like the one in the old picture book—the round window over the door like one big eye to watch. Her house—it *was!*

Now she cupped one hand protectingly around one dome and held the other out to Bim.

"A house," he said in blank surprise. "What's so special about a house?"

"It's *the* house," she told him with some of her old impatience. "The house I want—I wanted! See there's the eye window! And even the big step in front!"

Of course, though, Bim did not know *the* house. But he did not seem to be listening to her now. Instead—he turned the dome around viewing it from all sides. "You know, this's pretty neat —look at those windows—and . . . how could anybody make anything that small look so real?"

"I don't know—but it's yours—just like this one's mine."

"Hey!" Monnie was still enraptured with the house but Bim was pointing past her to the ground. "Hey—look what's happened to the mailbox!"

Monnie looked. It no longer stood upright but had fallen on its side, and there was a great rusty hole in it now, while the lid had disappeared and the flag was only a stub of bent metal.

"Nobody can use it again," Monnie said.

"They sure can't. Come on! Let's get going —this's plain spooky!"

Luck was with them. They got back to the project and into the apartment unseen. Monnie heard the stir of movement inside the Johnsons' bedroom. It was Sunday, she suddenly remembered. Stella would sleep late, but Mrs. Johnson would expect them to be ready for Sunday school. Bim, with the same idea in mind, scuttled into his own room as Monnie slipped into hers, taking care not to wake Stella.

She hid the tiny bubble-covered house at the bottom of her bureau drawer and tried to sort out the adventures of the night. A lot of it seemed like a dream now. But she thought she would never quite forget that other Monnie and all the shadows she had trailed with her. Maybe there could be more shadows added, if Monnie was not careful from now on. The broom, the doll, the mirror—they had all showed her something, something she must remember.

Bim stood by the window with the tiny house in his hand. The more he looked at it the more he wished he knew a real house like that. He wondered if it would disappear like the wand and the candle and the star had done. Fore some reason he hoped not. He crossed the room to stare into the mirror.

At least he was looking at himself—not that other Bim—or Bims, though he half-expected to see some of the shadowy ones at his back, or almost did. You could not run from what was inside you—you had to stop and face it. He nodded firmly at his reflection.

Both children were still lost in their own thoughts as they came to the breakfast table. Mrs. Johnson seemed unusually quiet, too. Then she said suddenly, as if this had to be said and she might as well get it over with:

"I—you'll stay home today and not go off anywhere later to play. There's going to be a change for you—the both of you. . . ."

Bim's head came up and his hand froze halfway to his mouth, tightening around the spoon

165

full of breakfast food. He knew it—he just knew it!

Monnie stared. She ought to be used to hearing that sort of thing by now, but she never was inside.

"They have a new program," Mrs. Johnson went on hurriedly. "It's a fine chance for both of you. It's a kind of home and school—together—and it's just starting. Miss Valasco and Miss Reeder both think you'll like it."

Bim chewed away on his cereal—the mouthful tasted like nothing at all. He was going to be moved on again. Monnie pushed away her plate. She was not hungry. Not now.

"You'll like it fine." Mrs. Johnson's words came faster and faster. "They've taken over the old Veneer place, out on Leonard Street. See?" She got up from the table and brought a paper which she put down so they both could see the picture of a house. "It's a real old house. You were asking, Monnie, about how old Veneer Street was just the other day, now weren't you? The Veneers—they were the first settlers here. They lived around here somewhere before they moved out and built their big house. It's not like the apartment but," Mrs. Johnson put more force in her voice with every word, "I know you'll like it. And it's a wonderful chance for you both. There will only be five of you—like a family. You'll like it. . . ." Her voice trailed off as if she were really begging them to agree, Monnie thought. Then she looked at that picture more closely.

The house! This was *the* house! Couldn't Bim see it too? They were going to live in *the* house!

He was frowning and leaning forward a little and then he shot a quick glance at Monnie. She nodded only a fraction but she saw that he understood.

"How long do you stay there?" he asked suspiciously.

"Until you're grown-up," Mrs. Johnson said eagerly, as if she welcomed questions, at least questions like that.

"No more changes?" Monnie wanted to be sure.

"No more," Mrs. Johnson agreed. "You see everything is working out just right. We've—well, we've been worried about things. Not that we have wanted to lose you—either of you—but we just didn't know what we were going to do. Ed and I, we have to go south—to live with Ed's brother who's sick. Stella wants to stay here and she's going to room with her friend Margaret. I don't know what we could have done. Only this chance for you came just at the right time." She put one finger on the pictured house and tapped it.

"Just at the right time," murmured Monnie. She was wildly impatient though she made herself sit there quietly. She wanted to see *the* house, she had to see *the* house! Inside, would it be what she always had wanted? It *must* be!

Bim took another spoonful of cereal. To get away, make a new start where he wouldn't be adding to those shadow Bims he had come to hate. Monnie—he could tell how excited she was. Well, maybe he was, too—just a little. No, not another lie, Bim—he was excited a whole lot!

This was the seventh spell and perhaps it was going to be the best of all!

## ABOUT THE AUTHORS

ANDRE NORTON is a highly-acclaimed and prolific writer of science fiction. She has had over seventy books published both in the United States and abroad, and her novels have appeared in several languages. Miss Norton has received numerous writing and science fiction awards, including the Gandalf Award for "Life's Work in Fantasy." She was the first woman writer to become a member of S.A.G.A. (Swordsmen and Sorcerers Guild). Her other Archway titles include *Star Ka'at, Star Ka'at World, Star Ka'at and the Plant People, Steel Magic, Fur Magic* and *Octagon Magic.*

PHYLLIS MILLER makes her debut as a novelist with *Seven Spells to Sunday,* a novel inspired by a young reader who asked for a book about "real magic." Mrs. Miller holds degrees from Case Western Reserve University and Fordham University, where she was a Graduate Scholar in Medieval History.